A
SINGLE
GLANCE

W WINTERS

I saw her from across the bar.
My bar. My city. Everything in that world belonged to me.
She stood out from the crowd, looking like she was
searching for someone to blame for her pain.

That night, I felt the depths of my mistakes and the
scars they left behind. With a single glance, I knew
her touch would take it all away and I craved that
more than anything.

I knew she would be a tempting, beautiful mistake.
One I would make again and again... even if it cost
me everything.

Dedicated to both TJ and Gem. In no particular order. Your love for my books and these characters knows no bounds. You have no idea how happy it makes me to hear you guys fighting over who licked Jase first. I love you both… and I'm staying out of this one!

MUAH!

A
SINGLE
GLANCE

PROLOGUE

Bethany

I'VE LEARNED TO LOVE THE COLD. TO LOVE THE heat that comes after. To love his touch. Whatever bit of it he'll give me.

Only when we're in this room though. Outside of it, he's still my enemy. And I'll never forget that. But when I'm tied down and waiting for him to use me as he wishes... I live for these moments.

The edge of the knife drags down my body, the blade running along my bare skin and taking the peach fuzz from every inch of me. It doesn't cause pain, but it leaves a sensitive trail that awakens every nerve ending it passes. Making me feel alive, so desperate and so conscious of how good it feels to long for something.

The knife travels down my collarbone carefully, meticulously, leaving a chill in the air that dares me to shiver as the sharp knife glides lower, down to the small mounds of my breasts. It's so cold when he's not hovering over me. The icy bite of the air alone has never brought pleasure, but knowing what's to come, the draft is nearly an aphrodisiac.

All the heat I need is buried between my legs, waiting for him to move the knife lower, bringing with it his hands, his breath… his lips.

The desire stirs deep in my belly, then lower still. With my legs spread just slightly, my thighs remain touching at the very top, closest to my most bared asset. The temperature in the room is low, low enough to turn my nipples to hardened peaks. Sometimes he drags the tip of his knife up to the top of my nipples, teasing me, and when he does this time, I let my head fall back, feeling the pleasure build inside of me. The smallest touches bring the largest thrills.

He tortures me just like this; he has for weeks. At one point, it did feel like suffering, but I crave it now. Every piece of it. I only feel lust when I think about being at his mercy.

"I love you naked on this bench." Jase's deep voice is so low, I barely hear him. But I feel his warm breath along my belly as he moves his tongue to run right where the blade has just been.

He does this first every time, teasing me with the knife, shaving any trace of hair before moving on. He always takes his time, and part of me thinks it's because he doesn't want this to end either. Once the flames have all flickered out and darkness sets in, and the loud click of the locks in the barren room signal it's over, that's when reality comes rushing back.

The war. The drugs. All of the lies that leave a tangled

web for me to get lost in.

I don't want any of it.

I want to swallow, the need is there, but I know to wait until the blade is lifted, leaving me cold and begging for it back on my skin. Teasing me. It's only once he pulls it back that I dare to swallow the lump in my throat and turn my head on the thick wooden bench to look at him.

Jase Cross.

My enemy. And yet, the only person I trust.

Fear used to consume me in these moments, but as the rough rope digs into my wrists, not an ounce of it exists. His dark eyes flicker, mirroring the flames of the fireplace lining the back wall of the room.

My gaze lingers as he swallows too, highlighting the stubble that travels from his throat up to his sharp jawline. That dip in his neck begs me to kiss him. Right there, right in that dip, as if he's vulnerable there.

With broad shoulders and a smoldering look in his dark eyes, Jase is a man born to be powerful. His muscles rippling in the fire's light as he looks down at me force my heart to flicker as well.

The gold flecks in his irises spark, and I'm lost in a trance. So much so that I freely admit what I never have before as I say, "I love it too."

I swear I see the hint of a smile tugging the corners of his lips up, but it's gone before I'm certain.

I shouldn't have said that. I shouldn't have given him more power than he already has.

Jase Cross will be my downfall.

CHAPTER
1

Jase
One month earlier

I T'S A SLOPPY MISTAKE. I NEVER MAKE A MISTAKE like this. *Never.* Yet, staring at the bit of blood still drying on my oxfords, I know I've made a mistake that could have cost me everything.

And it's all because of her. She's a distraction. A distraction I can't afford.

The thick laces run along my fingertips as I untie them, and as I do, a bit of blood stains my fingers. Pausing, I contemplate everything that could have happened if I hadn't seen it just now. I rub the blood between my fingers, then wipe it off with a napkin from my desk. Carefully, I slip off my shoes, shoving the napkin inside of one before grabbing a new pair from behind my desk and putting them on.

The pair with evidence of my latest venture will meet the incinerator before I leave my bar, The Red Room, tonight. Where all evidence is meant to be left.

"What do you think?" Seth asks me, and I turn my attention back to him. Back to the monitors.

She's gorgeous. That's what I think. With deep hazel eyes filled with a wild fire and full lips I'd silence easily with my own, even if she's screaming on the security footage, she's nothing but stunning.

Her anger is beautiful.

The bar and crowd would normally take my attention away from her, but I was there that night and I only saw her. The patrons from last week get in the way of seeing her clearly on the security footage though. I can barely make out her curves… but I do. Even if I can't fully see them here, I remember them. I remember everything about her.

If I hadn't been with my brother at the time and in a situation I couldn't leave, I would have been the one to go to her. Instead, I had Seth throw her out. No one was to harm her, which isn't the best example to set, but I wanted to tempt her to come back. I needed to see her again. If for nothing more than to serve as a beautiful distraction.

Running my thumb over the fleshy pads of my fingertips, I lean back in the chair, crossing my ankles under my desk and letting my gaze roam over every bit of her as he leads her out.

My voice is low, but calm as I comment, "She's different here than she is in the file."

"Anger will do that. She lost her fucking mind coming into your bar talking about calling the cops."

Although my lips kick up into an asymmetric smile, a

heaviness weighs down on me. There's too much shit going on right now for us to handle any more trouble.

She's a mistake waiting to happen. A delicate disaster in the making.

"How many days ago was this?" I ask, not remembering since the days have melded together in the hell that this past week was.

"Eight days; she hasn't come back."

"What do you want me to do?" Seth asks when I don't respond.

"Show me the footage again."

He's my head of security at The Red Room, and over the years I've come to trust him. Although, not enough to tell him what I really want from her. How seeing her defy the unspoken rules of this world, seeing her slander my name, curse it and dare me to do anything to stop her... I'm harder than I've been in a long fucking time.

"She's irate about her sister," Seth murmurs as the screen rewinds, then plays the footage of her parking her car, storming into the place, and demanding answers from a barkeep who doesn't know shit.

None of them could have given her the answer she wants.

I recognize every movement. The sharpness of her stride, the way her throat tenses before she even says a damn thing. I bet she can feel each of her words sitting on the tip of her tongue, threatening to silence her before she's even begun.

Even still, I find her beautiful. There is beauty in everything about what she did and how she feels.

"She lost her fucking mind," he mutters, watching

along with me.

Seth is missing something though, because he doesn't know what I know. He doesn't see it like I do.

She's not just angry; she's lonely. And more than that, she's scared.

I know all about that.

The days go by so slowly when you're lonely. They drag on and bring you with them, exaggerating each second, each tick of the clock and making you wonder what it's all worth.

I can't deny the ambition, the desire for more. There's always more. More money, more power, more to conquer. And with it more enemies and more distrust.

It's a predictable life, even amidst the chaos.

"I can understand why she's looking for someone to blame." I pause to move my gaze from the screen to Seth, and wait for him to look back at me. "But why us?" I ask him, emphasizing each word.

He shakes his head as he skims through the file he's holding, an autopsy report and photographs of a body catching my eye in particular, although you can barely tell that's what she was after washing up on shore. Dental records were needed to identify her, the poor woman.

"She thinks you and your brothers are responsible."

"No shit," I answer him, waiting for his attention before adding, "but why would she think that?"

Again he shakes his head. "There's nothing here that would lead her to that conclusion. We didn't touch the girl. Her sister wasn't a threat to anything that we know of."

My fingers rap on the desk as I think about Jennifer, the girl who died so tragically. I met her once, and I can imagine she got into far more trouble than she could handle.

"I'll figure it out, Boss," Seth tells me and I immediately answer, "Don't go to her."

His brow raises, but he's quick to fix the display of shock. "Of course," he replies.

"I'm arranging to see her shortly. Dig up everything you can on her and on her sister's death."

"Will do," Seth says as he slips the papers back into the folder and then glances at the monitors once again. The paused image of Beth shows her leaning across the bar midscream, demanding answers. Answers I don't have for her. Answers she may never get.

"The other reason I wanted to see you... I have those papers you wanted," Seth says, interrupting my thoughts.

"What papers?"

"The ones about your brother."

My brother.

There's always someone to fight. Someone to blame.

It never stops.

CHAPTER
2

Bethany

P EOPLE MOURN DIFFERENTLY. MY MOTHER
would turn in her grave if she knew I went to work
last night instead of going to my sister's funeral. My
sister, Jennifer, was the only family I had left.

And instead of watching Jenny be put in the ground,
beside my mother who's been there for a decade, I worked.

Yes, my mother would turn in her grave if she knew.

But that's because my mother had never been able to
stand on her own two feet whenever there was a loss, or
any day of the week, really. Let alone take on a sixteen-hour
shift to avoid the burial of a loved one. The last loved one
I had.

As I let out a flat sigh, remembering how she used to
handle things, I watch my warm breath turn to fog. It's not
even late, but the sun has set and the dark winter night

feels appropriate if nothing else.

The laughter coming from inside my house doesn't though.

My heart twists with a pain I loathe. *Laughter*. On a night like tonight.

Gripping the door handle a little harder than I need to, I prepare myself for what's on the other side.

Distant relatives chattering in the corner, and the smell of every casserole known to man invade my senses.

The warmth is welcoming as I close the door behind me without looking, only staring straight ahead.

Even as I lean my back against the cold door, no one sees me. No one stops their unremarkable conversations to spare me a glance. Bottles clink to my right and I turn just in time to see a group of my sister's friends toasting as they throw back whatever clear liquor is in their glasses. *My glasses*.

With a deep breath, I push off the door. Focusing on the sound of my coat rustling as I pull it off, I barely make eye contact with an aunt I haven't seen in years.

"My poor dear," she says, and I notice how her lips purse even while she's speaking. With a wine glass held away from her, she gives me a one-armed hug. "I'm so sorry," she whispers.

Everyone is so, so sorry.

Offering her a weak smile, and somehow not voicing every angry thought that threatens to strangle me, I answer back, "Thank you."

Her gaze drifts down to my boots, still covered with a light dusting of snow and then travels back up to my eyes. "Did you just get done with work?"

I lie. "Yes. Did the scrubs give it away?" The small joke eases the tension as she grips my shoulder. This isn't the first time I've ventured to the bar before coming home. Although, this is the first time the house isn't empty. And it's the first time I've felt I truly needed a drink. I need something to numb... *all of this*.

"Would you like a drink?" she offers me and then tells a group of people I've never met goodbye as they make their way out of my house.

"How about some red wine. A nightcap, since it's almost over?"

It's. Is she referring to the evening? Or the wake?

The tight smile on my face widens and I tell her, "I'd like that." My gaze wanders to the living room and I spitefully think that I'd like the four-year-old rummaging through the drawer of my coffee table to get out. They can all get out.

That thin smile still lingers on my lips when she brings me a glass and I nod a thanks, although I don't drink it. Not because I don't need one, but purely out of spite.

"Did the caterers bring everything?" I ask her politely, nodding a hello at a few family members who offer a pathetic wave in return. My mother was the black sheep of the family. Because of that, I couldn't name half of the people in here even though I recognize their faces. She got a divorce when my dad skipped out on us, and the family essentially divorced her for not "trying harder" in her marriage.

So the majority of the people here, I've met only once or twice... usually at funerals.

"They did," Aunt Margaret answers and I'm quick to

add, "I'm glad everyone could come."

I hate lies, but tonight they slip through my lips so easily. Even as the emotions make my throat swell up when I see the same group of girls doing another round of shots.

Maybe it makes me a hypocrite, seeing as how I just came from drowning myself in vodka and Red Bull at the bar down the street, Barcode. I tend to swing by after a lot of hard shifts, but that particular group doesn't need any more drugs added in the mix.

"The funeral was beautiful." My aunt's words bring a numbness that travels down my throat and the false expression I'm wearing slips, but I force the smile back on my face when she looks up at me.

I take a sip of cheap Cabernet and let the anger simmer. *Beautiful.*

What a dreadful word for a funeral.

For the funeral of a woman not yet thirty. A woman who none of these people spoke to. A woman I tried so desperately to save, because at one point in my life, she was my hero.

The glass hits the buffet a little harder than I wanted.

"Sorry I didn't make it. I'm glad it went well." My voice is tight.

"It was really kind of you to pay for everything... I know there's nothing in the estate or..." she says, but her voice drifts off, and I nearly scream at her. I nearly scream at all of them.

Why are they doing this? Why put on a front as if they cared? They didn't come to visit any of the times she was in the hospital. They didn't pay a cent for anything but their gas to attend the funeral and come here. And whatever those fucking casseroles cost. All the while I know they were gossiping, wondering about everything Jenny had done to land herself in an early grave.

They're from uptown New York and all they do is brag on social media about all their charity events. All their expensive dresses and glasses of champagne, put on full display every weekend for the charity that they so generously donated to.

I'm sure that would have been so much better.

Or maybe this alternative is their charity for the weekend. Coming to this fucking wake for a woman they didn't care about.

I could scream at myself as well; why open my door to these people? Why tell my aunt the reception could be held here? Was I still in shock when I agreed? Or was I just that fucking stupid?

They didn't see what happened to her. How she morphed into a person I didn't recognize. How my sister got sucked down a black hole that led to her destruction, and not a single one of them cared to take notice.

Yet they can comment on how beautiful her funeral was.

How lovely of them.

"Oh dear," my aunt says as she hugs me with both arms this time and I let her. The anger isn't waning, but it's not for them. I know it's not.

I'm sorry they didn't get to see those moments of her that shined through. The bits of Jenny that I'll have forever and they'll never know. I feel sorry for them. But her? My sister? I'm so fucking angry she left me here alone.

Everyone mourns differently.

The thought sends a peaceful note to ring through my blood as I hear footsteps approach. My aunt doesn't pull away, and I find myself slightly pushing her to one side and picking up a cocktail napkin to dry under my eyes.

"Hey, Beth." Miranda, a twentysomething string bean of a girl with big blue eyes and thick, dark brown hair, approaches. Even as she stands in front of me, she sways. The liquor is getting to her.

"Do you guys have a ride home?" I ask her, wanting to get that answer before she says anything else.

She blinks slowly, and the apprehension turns into hurt. She shifts her tiny weight from one foot to the other. Her nervousness shows as she tucks a lock of hair behind her ear, swallowing thickly and nodding. "Yeah," she croaks and her gaze drops to the floor as she bites the inside of her cheek. "Sorry about last time," she barely whispers before looking me in the eyes. "We've got a ride this time."

It's when she sniffles that I notice how pink her cheeks are – tearstained pink – not from drinking. Fuck, regret is a spiked ball that threatens to choke me as I swallow.

"I just don't want you guys getting into another accident, you know?" I get out the words quickly in a single breath, and pick up that glass of wine, downing it as Aunt Margaret turns her back on this conversation, leaving us for more... proper things maybe.

Miranda's quiet, looking particularly remorseful.

I don't mention how the accident was in front of my house, five fucking feet from where they were parked. Miranda passed out after getting drunk with Jenny and some other people nearby. Her foot stayed on the gas and revved her car into mine, pushing both cars into my neighbor's car until mine hit a tree. She could have killed them all. All four of them in the car, high and drunk and not caring about the consequences. Consequences for more than just them.

Her voice is small. "Yeah, I know. I'm sorry. It was a bad night."

A bad night? It was a bad month, and the start of me losing my sister. That night, I couldn't turn a blind eye to it any longer.

"I just wanted to say," she begins, but raises her voice a little too loud and then has to clear her throat, tears rimming her eyes. "I wanted to tell you I'm really sorry." Her sincerity brings my own emotions flooding back, and I hate it. "I loved your sister, and I'm…" This time I'm the one doing the hugging, the holding.

"Sorry," she rasps in a whisper as she pulls away. I look beyond her, at the groups of people in the dining room and past that to the kitchen. There are maybe twenty or thirty people in my house. And not a single one looks our way. They're too busy eating the food I paid for and drinking my alcohol. I wonder if they even feel this pain.

"She had this for you." Miranda pushes a book into my chest before running the sleeve of the thin sweater she's wearing under her eyes. Black mascara seeps into the light gray fabric instantly. "Right before she went missing, while she crashed at my place, she couldn't stop reading it."

It takes me a moment to actually take the book from her. It's thick, maybe a few hundred pages… with no cover. The spine's been torn off and my name replaces it. *Bethy*. That's what Jenny used to call me. The black Sharpie marker bled into the torn ridges of what the spine would have protected.

"What is it?" I ask Miranda, not taking my eyes from the book as I turn it over and look for any indication as to what story it is. I can feel creases in my forehead as my brow furrows.

Miranda only shrugs, the sweater falling off her shoulder and showing more of her pale skin and protruding collarbone. "She just kept saying she was going to give it to you. That you needed it more than her."

My gaze focuses on the first lines of the book, skimming them but finding no recollection of this tale in my memory. I have no idea what the book is, but as I flip through the pages, I notice some of the sentences are underlined in pen.

He loves like there's no reason not to. That's the first line I see, and it makes me pause until the conversation pulls me away.

"Before she died, she told me things." Miranda's large eyes stare deep into mine.

Jenny told me things too. Things I'll never forget. Warnings I thought were only paranoia.

As Miranda's thin lips part, my boss, Aiden, walks up to us in a tailored suit and Miranda shies back. My lips pull into a tight smile as he hugs me.

"You're dressed to the nines," I compliment him with a sad smile, not bothering to hide the pain in my voice. Miranda leaves me before I can say another word to her. She ducks her head, getting distance from me as quickly as she can. My eyes follow her as Aiden speaks.

"You okay?"

My head tilts and my eyes water as I reply, "Okay is

such a vague word, don't you think?"

He's older than me, and not quite a friend, but not just a boss either. The second my arms reach around his jacket, accepting his embrace, he holds me a little tighter and I hate how much comfort I get from it.

From something so simple. So genuine. My circle is small, but I like to keep it that way. And Aiden is one of the few people in it. He's one of the few people I can be myself with.

"I heard you didn't go... that it was today?" he asks me, although it's more of a statement, my face still pressed against his chest.

I won't cry. I won't do it.

Not until I'm alone anyway. I can't hide behind anger then. There's nowhere to hide when you're lying in bed by yourself.

"I couldn't bring myself," I tell him, intending on saying more, but my bottom lip wobbles and I have to pull away.

He's reluctant, but he lets me and I find my own arms wrapping around myself. Looking back to where Jenny's friends were, I notice they're gone, along with a lot of the crowd.

Maybe they heard my unspoken wishes.

"You need to take time off." Aiden's words shock me. Full-blown shock me.

My head shakes on its own and I struggle to come up with something to refute him. Money seems like the most logical reason, but Aiden beats me to it.

"There was a pool at work, and the other nurses are giving you some of their days for PTO. You have your own banked, plus the bereavement leave. And I know you have vacation time too."

"They don't have to do that…" My voice is low, full of disbelief. At Rockford, the local youth mental hospital, I know everyone more than I should, especially the night shift. But I wouldn't ever expect any of them to give me their time off. I don't expect anything from anyone.

"They can't do that. They'll need those days for themselves." They don't even know me really. I'm taken aback that they would do such a thing.

"It's a day here and a day there, it adds up and you need it."

"I'm fine-"

"My ass you are." Aiden's profanity draws my gaze to his, and the wrinkles around his eyes seem more pronounced. His age shows in this moment. "You need time off."

Time off.

More time alone.

"I don't want it."

"You're going to take it. You need to get your head on right, Fawn." His voice is stern as my body chills from a gust of air blowing into the dining room when my front door opens once again. More *guests* leaving.

"How many days?" I ask him, feeling defeat, so much of it, already laying its weight against me.

"You have six weeks," he informs me and it feels like a death sentence. My heart sinks to the pit of my stomach as my front door closes with a resounding click.

With his hands on my shoulders he tells me, "You need to get better."

Holding back the pain is a challenge, but I manage to breathe out with only a single tear shed. Six weeks.

The next breath comes easier.

I tell myself I'll take some time off, but not to get better.

My breathing is almost back to normal at my next thought.

But to find the men responsible for what happened to my sister.

☯☯

My eyes are burning and heavy, but I can't sleep.

I'm exhausted and want to lie down, but my legs are restless and my heart is wide awake, banging inside of me. I need to do something to take this agony away. Staring back at The Coverless Book beside me on the side table, I lean to the left, flicking on the lamp while still seated on my sofa.

The Coverless Book
Prologue

I'm invincible. I tell myself as I pull the blanket up tighter.

My heart races, so fast in my chest. It's scared like I am.

Jake is coming.

He's going to see me here in my house, and then where could I possibly hide from him? Where could I hide my blush?

Maybe behind this blanket?

"Miss?" Miss Caroline calls into the room, and I perk up.

"Yes?"

"Your guest is here," she announces and I give her a nod, feeling that heat rise to my cheeks and my heart fluttering as she gives me a knowing smile and I hide my brief laugh. Caroline knows all my secrets.

Before I can stand up on shaky legs, he's standing in the doorway, tall and lanky as most eleventh-graders are. But Jake is taller. His eyes softer. His hands hold a shock in them that gets me every time he reaches for my calculator in class.

"Jake." His name comes from me in surprise as I struggle to lift myself.

"Emmy." The way he says my name sounds so sad. "I heard you were sick."

⟨∅⟩∅⟩

I read the prologue and the first chapter too before falling asleep on the old sofa that used to belong to my mother. I'm cocooned in the blanket I once wrapped my sister in when the drugs she'd taken made her shake uncontrollably.

The only sentence Jenny underlined was the one that read, "I'm invincible."

Jenny, I wish you had been. I wish I were too.

CHAPTER
3

Bethany

M Y EYES FEEL SO HEAVY. SO DRY AND
itchy.

Rubbing them only makes it hurt worse.

I would have slept better had I worked. I know I
would have.

My gaze drifts back to the book. I'm only a few chapters in, but I keep walking away from the pages, not remembering where I left off and starting over each time.

Knowing I can't focus on work, knowing it's been
taken away, has brought out a different side of me.

The side that remembers my sister.

Not the way she was in the last few years, but the way
she was when we were younger.

When we were thick as thieves, and my older sister
was my hero. Those memories keep coming back every

time I read the chapters written from Emmy's perspective. She's young, and sweet, but so damn strong. My sister was strong once. Held down by no one.

Once upon a time.

Letting out a deep breath, I stretch my back, pushing the torn-up book onto my coffee table. I sit there, looking out the front bay window of my house. The curtains are closed, but not tightly and I catch a glimpse of a car pull up.

A nice car. An expensive one.

All black with tinted windows. Jenny came home in a car like that once, shaken and crying. Back when all of her troubles started. My blood runs cold as the car stops in front of my house.

If it's someone she was associated with, I don't want them here.

Anger simmers, but it's futile. You can only be angry for so long.

Once it's gone, fear has a way of creeping into its place.

My pace is slow, quiet and deliberate as I head to my coat closet and reach up to a backpack I haven't used in years. I figured it would be the perfect place to hide the gun. The one Jenny brought home for me, the one she said I needed when she wouldn't listen to me and refused to stay. I was screaming at her as she shoved it into my chest and told me I needed to take it.

It was only weeks ago that my sister stood right here and gave me a gun to protect myself, when she was the one who needed help. She needed protecting.

Jase

I can't handle one more thing going wrong.

My keys jingle as the ignition turns off and the soft rumble of the engine is silenced.

Wiping a hand over my face, I get out of the car, not caring that the door slams as my shoes hit the pavement. The neighborhood is quiet and each row of streets is littered with picture-perfect homes, nothing like the home I grew up in. Little townhouses of raised ranches, complete with paved driveways and perfectly trimmed bushes. A few houses have fences, white picket of course, but not 34 Holley, the home of Bethany Fawn.

Other than the missing fence, the two-story home could be plucked straight from an issue of *Better Homes & Gardens*.

Knock, knock, knock. She's in there; I can hear her. Time passes without anything save the sound of scuttling behind the door, but just as I'm about to knock again, the door opens a few inches. Only enough to reveal a glimpse of her.

Her chestnut hair falls in wavy locks around her face. She brushes the fallen strands back to peek up at me.

"Yes?" she questions, and my lips threaten to twitch into a smirk.

"Bethany?"

Her weight shifts behind the door as her gaze travels down the length of my body and then back up before she answers me.

The amber in her hazel eyes swirls with distrust as she tells me, "My friends call me Beth."

"Sorry, I'm Jase. Jase Cross. We haven't met before... but I'll happily call you Beth." The flirtatious words slip from me easily, and slowly her guard falls although what's left behind is a mix of worry and agony. She doesn't answer or respond in any way other than to tighten her grip on the door.

"Mind if I have a minute?"

She purses her full lips slightly as the cracked door opens just an inch more, enough for her to cautiously reply, "Depends on what you're here for."

My pulse quickens. I'm here to give her a single warning. Just one chance to stay the hell away from The Red Room and to get over whatever ill wishes she has for my brothers and me.

It's a shame, really; she's fucking gorgeous. There's an innocence, yet a fight in her that's just as evident and even more alluring. Had I met her on other terms, I would do just about anything to get her under me and screaming my name.

But after this past week with Carter and all that bullshit, I made my decision. *No distractions.*

The swirling colors in her eyes darken as her gaze dances over mine. As if she can read my thoughts, and knows the wicked things I'd do to her that no one else ever could. But that's not why I'm here, and my perversions will have to wait for someone else.

I lean my shoulder against her front door and slip my shoe through the gap in the doorway, making sure she can't slam it shut. Instead of the slight fear I thought would flash in her eyes as my expression hardens, her eyes narrow with hate and I see the gorgeous hue of pink in her pale skin brighten to red, but not with a blush, with animosity.

"You need to stay out of the Cross business, Beth." I lean in closer, my voice low and even. My hard gaze meets her narrowed one, but she doesn't flinch. Instead she clenches her teeth so hard I think they'll crack.

With the palm of my hand carefully placed on the doorjamb and the other splayed against her door, I lean in to tell her that there are no answers for her in The Red Room. I want to tell her that my brother isn't the man she's after, but before I can say a word she hisses at me, "I know all about Marcus and the drugs and why you assholes had her killed."

The change in her tone, her expression is instant.

My pulse hammers in my ears but even over it, I hear the strained pain etched in her voice. Her breathing shudders as she adds, "You'll all pay for what you did to my sister." Her voice cracks as her eyes gloss over and tears gather in the corners of her eyes.

"You don't know what you're talking about," I tell her as the rage gathers inside of me. *Marcus*. Just the name makes every muscle inside of my body tighten and coil.

The drugs.

Marcus.

Before I can even tie what she's said together, I hear the click of a gun and she lets the door swing open, throwing me off-balance.

Shock makes my stomach churn as the barrel of a gun flashes in front of my eyes. She leans back, moving to hold the heavy metal piece with both hands.

Fuck! Lunging forward, still unsteady as dread threatens to take over, I grip the barrel and raise it above her head, shoving her small body back until it hits the wall in her foyer and she continues to struggle, pushing away from me and getting out of my grasp.

Bang!

The gun goes off and the flash of heat makes the skin of my hand holding the barrel burn and singe with a raw pain. Her lower back crashes into a narrow table, a row of books toppling over and a pile of mail falling onto the floor as I stumble into her and finally pin her to the wall.

My chest rises and falls chaotically. My body temperature heats with the adrenaline racing through me.

Her small shriek of terror is muted when I bring my right hand to her delicate throat. My left still grips the gun. I can't swallow yet, I can't do anything but press her harder against the wall, smothering the fight in her as best as I can.

She struggles beneath me, but with a foot on her height and muscle she couldn't match no matter how hard she tried, it's pointless. Her heart pounds hard, and I feel it matching mine.

"Knock it the fuck off," I grit between my teeth.

She yelps as I lift the gun higher, ripping it from her grasp. Both of her hands fly to the one I have tightening on her throat. On instinct, like I knew she would. Did she really think she could get one over on me?

"You tried to shoot me." I practically snarl the words, although they're nearly inaudible.

Struggling to catch my breath, I don't let anything show except the absolute control I have over her. The door is wide open and I'm certain someone could have heard, although it's a Monday and during work hours. It's why I chose this time to pay her a visit.

A faint breeze carries in from behind and I take a step back, pulling her with me just enough so I can kick the door shut and then press her back to the wall. Her pulse slows beneath my grip and her eyes beg me for mercy as her sharp nails dig into my fingers.

The way she looks at me, her hazel eyes swirling with a mix of pain, fear and anger still, makes my chest ache for her, because I see something else. Something that fucking hurts.

She doesn't want mercy. She wants it to end. I can see it so clearly. I've seen it before, and the unwanted memory is jarring in this moment.

A second passes before I loosen my grip just enough so she can breathe freely.

Through her frantic intake, I lean forward, crushing my body against hers until she's still. Until her eyes are wide and staring straight into mine. The sight of her, the fear, the desperation... I know I'm not letting her go. Not yet.

"You're going to tell me everything you know about Marcus." I lower my lips to the shell of her ear, letting my rough stubble rub along her cheek. "And everything you know about the drugs."

My mind is whirling with every reason I should walk away. Every reason I should simply kill her and leave this mess behind. She tried to kill me; that's reason enough.

But I don't want to. I need more.

With a steadying breath, my lungs fill with the sweet smell of her soft hair that brushes against my nose.

I comb my fingers through her hair and let my thumb

run along her slender neck before I lean into her, letting her feel how hard I am just to be alive. Just to have her at my mercy.

"And because of that little stunt you just pulled, I'm not letting you go."

CHAPTER
4

Jase

F*UCK!* THE PALM OF MY HAND BANGS ON THE steering wheel, sending a sharp pain radiating up my arm. Fuck! Over and over I slam my hand against the wheel while gritting my teeth to keep from screaming out profanities.

Even with the adrenaline still racing and the anger still present, I force myself to sit back in the car, listening to the dull thuds coming from the trunk.

I shouldn't have done that. *What the fuck was I thinking?*

I put cuffs around her wrists, her ankles too, and then gagged her to keep any more screams for help from crying out between those beautiful lips of hers.

I backed my car into her garage and dealt with the kicks and her feeble attempt to fight back as I forced her into the tight space.

I can only imagine what she's thinking with the hand-cuffs digging into her wrists as she's trapped, dark and alone and having no idea what's going to happen.

Thump. The sound reminds me—I shouldn't have done that shit.

Her garage door opens with an abrupt, jerky motion and then slowly rises, bringing with it a vision of the sub-urban street, lit by the warm glow of the inevitable evening. A sarcastic huff leaves my lips as I pull away, gently stepping down on the gas and blending in.

Knowing she's bound and gagged in the trunk, unable to do a damn thing until I decide what to do with her, time slips by as I drive down her street, thinking about how the hell I'm going to fix this shit.

The second I give her freedom again, she'll go to the cops, which is fine, since they're in our back pocket.

Every way I look at this, I know she's going to have to go. A threat is a threat is a threat. I underestimated her, but now that I know what she's willing to do, there's no excuse for keeping her alive.

No reason except for that look in her eyes.

The blinker ticks as I round the corner, turning right out of her neighborhood and down the main drag. I'm not taking her to the back of The Red Room. I don't want a damn soul to know about her pulling out a weapon. She's merely a nuisance, nothing more.

No one can know. If they find out and I don't silence her, they will.

"Call Seth." I give the command and instantly the cabin of the sedan fills with the sound of a phone ringing. Before it finishes the second ring, Seth answers.

"Boss," he greets me.

"I need you to do something."

"I'm listening." I can hear the shuffle of papers in the background and then it goes quiet on the other line.

"Drive out to the address you gave me yesterday. You know which one?" I ask him and keep my words vague. I'm careful not to risk a damn thing, not when calls can be recorded and used against me.

"Of course," he answers and I can practically see him nodding his head in the way that he does. Short and quick, with his eyes never leaving mine.

"I went over there and I may have made a mess."

"Just clean it up?" he asks. "Anything in particular to look out for?"

"The hinge on her door broke, and there's a bullet hole in her ceiling, but everything's fine otherwise. No one will be there, so lock it on your way out." A thought hits me as I get closer to my own home and my fingers slide down to my house key, dangling from the ignition. "I'm going to need you to make me a copy of a key too."

"For the address I gave you yesterday?" he clarifies and I nod while answering, "Yes."

"Anything else?" he asks and I'm silent for a moment, thinking about the next step and the one after it.

Seth is a fixer. Every fuckup I make, or better yet, any fuckups from my brothers, he cleans up. He's also my right-hand man when I want to keep things from Carter.

"If anyone asks or comes looking, let them know you were hired to fix it."

"No problem."

31

Thump, thump, THUMP! My gaze lifts to the rearview mirror as I listen to Beth trying to escape. The trunk can't be opened from the inside; she'll learn I'm smarter than that. She caught me off guard once, but it won't happen again.

CHAPTER
5

Bethany

M Y HEART WON'T STOP RACING. IT'S
pounding hard and fighting back from inside
my chest; I can't imagine I'll survive this.

It's throbbing so loud, it takes me a moment to realize the car's stopped. The hum of the engine has vanished
and there isn't a damn sound other than my own chaotic
heartbeat.

I hear a crunch, I think, and my head whips around
to the side, so sharply it sends a bolt of pain down my already aching shoulder. Traveling up and down my shoulders is a dull fire that blazes. Between the way I was forced
in here, practically thrown in, and lying on my arms with
them cuffed behind my back, my shoulders are in absolute
agony. The metal bites into my wrists and ankles, and I
know I'll have bruises on my knees from slamming them

as hard as I could into the top of the trunk. My entire body is cramping.

Every trunk has a latch somewhere on the inside. It's to save children from being locked within and trapped. I know because I once played hide-and-seek with my sister and tried to get in the trunk, only to have my mother scream at me. She said it was dangerous, and the neighbor girl we were playing with told my mother what her mother had told her. That there was a latch on the inside. Sure enough, there was. My mother still didn't let me hide in the trunk though and after she grabbed me by the hand and brought me inside, I didn't want to play anymore.

Since being dumped in here, I've spent all my energy maneuvering through the pain to search for the latch. I can't fucking find it. So I resorted to bucking my body in a desperate attempt to force the trunk open or to kick out a taillight. Anything. Anything at all to get the hell out of here.

No luck. And now it's too late.

It's funny what you think of while you're waiting for the inevitable. Maybe it's a coping mechanism, a way to take your mind elsewhere when darkness is looming. Or maybe my memory was simply triggered by the lack of a handle and how I learned such a thing should be here because of hide-and-seek. Maybe that's why as I close my eyes and listen for something, for anything at all, my mind takes me elsewhere. I hear my sister call my name down the hall of our childhood home.

I'm in the closet upstairs, and it's so hot. I buried myself under all the blankets my mother stored on the floor in there and carefully laid them on top of me, hoping that when Jenny opened the door, searching for me, she wouldn't see me.

She was always better than me at everything—every game, every sport, every class. But today, when she opened that door, and I waited with bated breath, she closed it and continued silently searching the house.

With the smugness to keep me company, I stayed there under those blankets and I must have fallen asleep. It was Jenny's voice that woke me and when I came to, I felt so hot. I was absolutely drenched in sweat and the blankets felt so much heavier than they did before.

"Jenny," I cried out for her, feeling an overwhelming fear that didn't seem to make sense, but I knew I needed to get out from under the blankets. I couldn't shove them forward though, the door was closed and I couldn't lift them up because a shelf was above me. "Jenny!" I cried out again. Louder this time, as I tried to wiggle my way free under the weight of the pile. I didn't have to free myself alone though; Jenny opened the door and helped me out, telling me I was okay all the while and when I did crawl out into the hallway, I knew I was okay, but it didn't feel like I was.

I never hid there again. I don't think I ever played hide-and-seek again at all.

There's another loud crunch, and another. My eyes pop open and suddenly I am very much in the present, leaving the memory behind. I'm listening to the sound of shoes walking along small pieces of gravel maybe. The beating in my chest intensifies and I can't breathe as I hear the steps get closer. I even squeeze my eyes shut, wishing I could make myself disappear, or go somewhere else. Like I used to do when I was a child. As if this could all just be a dream or I had somehow gained impossible abilities.

I would try to scream, but the balled-up shirt in my mouth is already threatening to choke me as every small movement sends it farther into my mouth. Any farther, and I think I'll throw up.

When the trunk swings open so loud that my instincts force me to look up, the light's bright, almost blinding.

I wish I could beg; I wish I could yell. I wish I could fight back when I see him towering over me and taking his time to consider me.

"That looks like it hurt," he says as if he finds it funny. The words come out with condescension as he reaches down to let his fingertips glide over my already bruised knees. Even the small movement makes me buckle, forcing my weight back onto my shoulders and it starts a series of aches cascading throughout my body all over again.

The agony begs me to cry, but in place of tears, I find myself screaming the words, "Fuck you," over the gag in my mouth. The soft cotton nearly touches the back of my throat, and for a moment I think, if I were to vomit right now, I'd choke on it.

I won't die like this. Not like this.

My gaze doesn't leave his as he angles his head, reaching up to grip the hood of the trunk with both of his hands. The sun's gone down and wherever we are, there are trees. Lots of trees.

Staring up at him, searching for a clue as to where we are, it's hopeless. Yellow light slips through the crisp dead leaves above us, giving way to a deep blue sky that'll soon turn to black night, and there isn't a damn thing else to see.

Nothing but his handsome face, and the way his broad shoulders pull that jacket a little too tight.

Let him think you've given up. Don't die like this. Use him. Use him to find out what happened to your sister.

The voice in my head comes out as a hiss. And with the reminder of Jenny, tears prick at my eyes. Through the glossy haze, I see the man's expression change. Jase's hardness, his cockiness, it all dims to something else.

My breathing slows, and the adrenaline wanes.

My fight isn't over, but I'll give in for now.

"We're going to have a conversation, Bethany." Jase's words sound ominous and they come with a cold gust of wind from the late fall air. Both send a chill down my spine and leave goosebumps in their wake.

"Nod if you understand." His hardened voice rises as he gives me the command. Loathing him and everything he stands for, I keep perfectly still, feeling the rage take over anything else. His eyes blaze with anger as he grips the hair at the nape of my neck, pulling my head back with a slight sting of pain and forcing me to look at him. "You need to play nice, Bethany." If I could punch him in the throat right now, I would. That's how *nice* I'm willing to play.

He lowers his head into the darkness of the trunk, sending shadows across his face that darken his stubbled jaw and force his piercing gaze to appear that much more dominating.

A heat flows in my blood as my breathing stutters and he brings his lips down to my neck. They gently caress my skin and with the simple touch, a spark ignites down my body. A spark I hate even more than I hate Jase himself.

His next words come with a warm breath and another tug at the base of my skull as he whispers, "You're going to listen to me, Bethany. You're going to do what I tell you... *everything* I tell you." The way he says the word everything dulls the heat, replacing it with fear, and for the first time, I truly feel it down to my bones. Standing up a little straighter, but still keeping his grip on me, he asks with a low tone devoid of any emotion, "We're going to have a conversation, isn't that right?" He loosens his grip on the back of my neck as he waits for my response.

I wish his gorgeous face was still close to mine, so I could slam my head into his nose.

With a tremor of fear running through me and that image of him rattling in my head, I nod.

As a small smile drifts along his lips and he nods his head in return, I welcome the cold gust that travels into the trunk.

He may think he can use me, but I swear to everyone, living and dead, I'll be the one using him.

CHAPTER
6

Bethany

H OPE IS A LONG WAY OF SAYING GOODBYE.
I told that to Jenny a few weeks ago. No, it was longer than that. It doesn't matter when, because by then, I'd lost my faith in her. Disappearing for days on end and talking about a man who had what she needed … my sister was never going to get help. I begged her to come back home, and she just shook her head no, and told me to hold on to hope.

I wanted her to stay with me. To get better.

I could have helped her, but you can't help those who don't want to be helped.

I can still feel her fingers, her nails just barely scratching the skin down my wrist as I ripped my hand away.

The memory haunts me as I think in this moment – this terrifying moment of waiting for his next move - I think, *I need to have hope that it's not over*. I need to have hope that I can get the fuck away from this man. That I can make him pay if he had any part in her death. *Jase Cross will fucking pay.*

The last thought strengthens my resolve.

"You'll be quiet," he tells me as if he's certain of it, a hint of a threat underlying each syllable, and I nod.

I nod like a fucking rag doll and try not to show how much it hurts when he rips the duct tape off my face in one quick tug. The stinging pain makes me reflexively reach for my mouth, but I can't; that act only exacerbates the cuts in my wrists, still cuffed behind my back. I try not to heave when he pulls the wet cloth from my mouth, finally giving me the chance to speak, to scream, to fucking breathe.

My body trembles; it's not from a cold breeze or the temperature though, and not from the fear I know is somewhere inside of me. Instead it's from the anger.

His eyes stay fixed on mine as he reaches down and lifts me into his chest before heaving me over his shoulder.

My teeth grit as he slams the trunk shut, turning to the side and giving me a view of a forest. All I see is a gravel drive and trees. So many trees. My heart gallops, both with that tinge of fear and with hope. *I could run.*

Fuck that.

I'm not running. I'm not giving up this chance to find out more about the family name I've heard so much about lately.

Somewhere in the back of my mind, I see my sister, and I hear her too. *The Cross brothers*, she whispers. She mentioned them so many times on the phone. He knew her. Or one of his brothers did.

As time stands still while I wait for the verdict I'm about to receive and what this man has in store for me, I remember the week my sister first went missing. I started with Miranda to try to figure out where my sister had gone. It made the most sense because Jenny told me she'd crash at a friend's place whenever we got into a fight. Miranda and she were close. But Miranda didn't have any idea what happened to her, only that she went out for drinks at The Red Room before she disappeared, a place I'd heard Jenny mention before. A place I knew I was headed to next.

All I had were two names and a single location. One name, Marcus, proved elusive—no one had any information on him at all. Not a single person inside The Red Room had any idea who he was. They wanted a last name, and I didn't have one. He was a dead end.

I'd spent hours at that bar, waiting for something. Waiting for anything. Any sign of her, or for anyone who knew them. Everyone knew of Jase, but no one *knew* him. They couldn't tell me anything about him. Nothing more than the dirt I dug up online.

They said he was one of the Cross brothers. The owner of The Red Room.

They said you don't cross a Cross; they laughed when they said it, like it was funny. Nothing was funny to me then.

And when two men appeared from the back of the club, heading toward a side entrance, the woman next to me pinched my arm and pointed as the side door was opened for them.

"Those are the Cross brothers," she said and then bit down on her bottom lip as she sucked it into her mouth.

She was skinny like a model, with the straightest black hair I'd ever seen. Her icy blue eyes never left the two of them and I stared at her for far too long, missing my chance to catch the Cross brothers. The thick throng of people kept me from making it to them, and by the time I got outside, they were nowhere in sight.

I stalked that place for four days straight, waiting for Jenny to show up. An aching hollowness in my heart reminds me how it felt, sitting there alone at the bar, praying she'd walk up to me or someone would message me that they found her.

It was late on that last night, and hopelessness was counting on me to give up so it could take over, but I never would.

It was 1:00 a.m.; I remember it distinctly because I had an early shift the next morning, and I kept thinking I wouldn't make it through my twelve-hour shift if I stayed out any later.

All the time I'd spent in the bar hadn't given me any new information. Countless hours had been wasted, but I didn't know what else to do or where else to go.

It was that night I got a better view of Jase. Only his silhouette, but it grabbed my attention and held me in place. The strength in his gaze, accompanied with a charming smile. He was handsome and beautiful even. I remember thinking he was the kind of man who could lure you in so easily and you wouldn't know what hit you ... until he was gone. He had that pull to him, a draw that made you want to go to him just to see if he'd look your way.

He came and he went and I sat on that stool, knowing my sister wasn't coming.

That was then. This is now.

A grunt of pain slips from me as he hoists me up higher on his shoulder, one hand wrapped around my waist to keep my body from falling backward, and the other hand swinging easily at his side.

Every step hurts, and the agony tears through me with my hands still restrained behind my back. Biting down on my bottom lip, I don't scream, and I don't try to fight him. Not like this.

I'll be good until I'm uncuffed. Then this fucker will get what he has coming to him.

His hand splays on my ass, immediately heating my core as I hear the jingle of keys. Craning my neck, I get the first view of where he's taken me.

A house in the forest. A big fucking house, to boot. It's three stories with white stone leading all the way up. My body reacts on its own; the need to run takes over, as if I could still run, cuffed like I am.

"Don't struggle." Jase's words come out hard, and I bite down harder on the inside of my cheek to keep from telling him to go fuck himself. If I could struggle, really struggle, I would.

He holds me tighter with both of his hands this time, and the sharp metal of the keys digs into my thigh. Even when I keep myself perfectly still, he doesn't let go.

With a tight throat and resentment flowing through my veins I attempt to answer him, but I can't think of anything to say. Maybe it's the blood pooling in my head, or maybe it's the pain finally taking over, but I have to close my eyes just to keep from passing out. The moment I do, he takes his hand away and I hear the keys scrape into the lock along with a beep from something that startles my eyes open, followed by the telltale sound of a door opening.

The beep… There's some sort of alarm beyond the key. It's then that I see my purse swinging. He brought it with him, and I force myself to think about everything in that bag that can be used as a weapon.

Knowing that and gathering information keeps me calm. Anything that can help me fight.

The warmth is welcoming, even as I bid farewell to the forest that leads somewhere to freedom. I intend for the goodbye to be temporary anyway.

I don't expect him to be careful as he sets me down in what looks like a foyer. But he is.

Thud. My heart flinches as the jangle of keys being tossed somewhere to my right hits me. And then I see him again.

His back is to me as he removes his jacket, revealing more of him. Everything is in place. The cuff links, the neatly trimmed hair on the back of his neck. He screams wealth, power… sex appeal.

My eyes close slowly at the thought, hating myself for recognizing that primal urge. They open just as slowly when his footsteps grab my attention. Even the sound of his steps hints of elite status. He walks toward me and my eyes stay on his, even though the depth of his stare dares me to defy him.

My stupid heart races, dying to get away.

He makes me feel weak and I hate him for it.

"I hate you." The hoarse words come from my throat unbidden. The fact that they only make him smirk as he crouches in front of me, pisses me off that much more. It hurts, though. I can't deny it does more than aggravate me to be at the mercy of this man.

Craning my neck and straightening my back so I can bring my eyes to his level only forces more weight onto my hands.

I seethe through clenched teeth, giving away the pain and that's when he breaks his stare.

I turn away from him to my right as he reaches behind me and uncuffs my hands first. He reaches for the pair on my ankles, but pauses.

"How much?" he asks me, his voice deep and husky.

My gaze flickers to his as I pull my hands into my chest, my fingers gripping around the small cuts, trying to rub some feeling back into my wrists. I hesitate only for a moment, confused by his question. "How much what?"

"How much do you hate me?" he asks, and my heart does it again. It scrambles in my rib cage, wanting so desperately to escape. The heart is a wild thing, meant to be caged after all.

I try to swallow, swallow down the spiked lump, but I can hardly do it. Staring into his eyes, I answer him, "It depends."

"On what?" he asks, letting his fingers drift over the metal cuffs, his eyes roaming from mine down my body. He tilts his head, looking back at me once again when I answer, "Whether you tell me the truth or not."

Thump, thump. My heart hates me.

"You're in no position to question me."

"What makes you think I'm not?" Somehow my words come out evenly; controlled and daring. I revel in it as his dark eyes flash with the heat of a challenge, but then he

45

moves his hand away from the cuffs, the small key still resting in his palm.

I could try to reach for it, but I wait.

When he peers down at me, I stare back without flinching, but the second his eyes are off of me, my gaze scatters across every inch of this place. Every window, every door. Every way out.

"You're not getting out of here until I let you out," Jase says absently when he catches me. So casually, as if he doesn't care.

My lips purse as I wait for more from him. If he thinks I won't try to get out, he's dead fucking wrong.

"You don't believe me?" he asks with a trace of humor lingering in his tone. I can feel my heartbeat slow, my blood getting colder with each passing second.

"There's always a way out." My words come out low, barely spoken, but he hears them and shakes his head before crouching in front of me again.

"Every window and door requires a fingerprint and a code, Bethany." The way he says my name sounds sinful on his tongue. I wish he'd take it back. I don't want him to speak my name at all.

My jaw clenches as I take in this new information and then ask him, "What do you want from me? Are you going to kill me?" The second question catches in my throat.

He runs the pad of his thumb along his stubbled jaw and then up to his lips, bringing my eyes to the movement as he says, "I went to your house with decent enough intentions. I wanted to tell you that you weren't going to get anywhere and whatever rabbit you were chasing was only going to lead you down a dead-end road and get you hurt, or worse."

I have to grab on to my fingers, squeezing them as tight as I can to keep from slamming my fists into his chest, to keep from slapping him or from punching him in his fucking throat as he gets closer to me.

"I don't have the answers you're looking for. I'm sorry about your sister," he says and my stomach drops, it drops so quickly and so low I feel sick. "I don't know how she died and I sure as shit didn't play a part in her death…" He pauses and inches closer to me, a hint of sympathy playing at his lips before he adds, "She owed us far too much money for me to kill her."

Dread is all-consuming as he stands, leaving me with a chill and turning his back to me. "I was being nice, giving you a warning and then you tried to shoot me."

He takes three steps away, three short steps while staring down at his own shoes as if contemplating. The hard marble floors feel colder and more unforgiving as I struggle with whether or not I believe him.

He's a bad man. Jase Cross, all of the Crosses are bad men. I don't believe him. I believe what Jenny told me.

She'd said the name Cross over and over again. Cross and The Red Room were my only real clues to go by. At that thought, there's a prickle at the back of my neck and I struggle to stay calm as the exhaustion, the sorrow, and the hate war with each other.

"I don't believe you," I whisper weakly but with his back to me, he doesn't hear me.

"I'll be nice again. Only because you remind me of someone I once knew." Looking up through my lashes, I wait for him to continue.

His dark eyes pierce me, seeing through me and causing both the need to beg for mercy and the need to spit on him, simply for not having the answers I crave.

"If you're lying to me… you'll pay," I utter and keep going. "I'll… I'll," I attempt a threat, but my last word cracks before I can finish.

Without warning, Jase closes the distance between us in foreboding steps I both loathe and refuse to be intimidated by. So I react. All I've been doing is reacting. I spit in his face the second he lowers himself to tell me off.

The shock from what I did is enough to outweigh the fear as Jase wipes his face, his expression morphing into fury as he stares at my spit in his hand.

Before I can say anything, he grips my throat. His large, hot hand wraps tightly around my neck, and my own hands reach up to his in a feeble attempt to rip his fingers off of me.

The heat from his body engulfs my own as I struggle to breathe. My nails dig into his fingers. His body is heavy against me, practically burning me. His entire being overshadows mine with power.

"I'll allow you to ask questions," he says and pauses, letting the air leave my lungs and the panic starts to take over, thinking there's no air to fill them, "but you will never," he pauses again for emphasis, staring into my eyes as they burn while he concludes, "threaten me again." Small lines form at the corners of his eyes as he narrows them, gazing at me and squeezing just a little tighter. So tight it hurts, and I struggle, scratching at my own throat in an effort to pry his grip loose.

My head feels light as my body sways in his grasp.

Just as I think he's going to kill me, that I'll die like this, he releases me.

Heaving in deep gulps of air, my shoulders hunch over.

I practically suffocate on the sudden rush of oxygen. My clammy palms hit the cold floor and my body rocks on its own.

"Don't make me regret this, Bethany." He does it again, saying my name like he had to spit it out of his mouth.

I grind my teeth against one another so hard that my jaw aches from the pressure. I have to stare intently at the spiral staircase behind him to keep from saying anything.

Time passes, the ticking of my heart somehow finding its normal rhythm once again in the silence.

"Your sister owed a debt, and you're going to pay it."

CHAPTER
7

Jase

L IES. I HEAR THE WORD IN MY HEAD OVER THE
sound of the armoire crashing to the bedroom floor.
I turn the speakers down, but continue to watch her
trash the guest bedroom.

I'm not surprised she's destroying everything she can.

As I dragged her to the guest bedroom, she never
stopped fighting, and I never stopped hearing the hiss in
my head. *Lies*.

Never tell a lie, my younger brother, Tyler, once told
me. I was fucking around with him about something when
we were kids. I don't remember what, but he looked up at
me and the words he spoke stuck with me forever.

A lie you have to remember. So never lie, it will only
fuck you over.

I can still see the smug look grow on his face as I felt

the weight of his words. He was an old soul and had a good heart. *Never tell a lie*. He'd be ashamed of the man I became.

The screaming that comes from the faint sound of the speakers brings me back to now, back to the present where I keep fucking up.

One mistake after the other, falling like dominos.

I stare at her form on the screen as she pounds her fists against the door, screaming to be let go. Bethany Fawn's throat is going to hurt tonight. It already sounds sore and raw from her fighting.

It's useless. Part of me itches to hit the release on her door to let her roam throughout my wing, struggling with every locked window, with the doors that will never open for her. Just to prove a point.

I can't blame her though and as she falls to her knees, violently wiping away the tears under her eyes as if they're a badge of dishonor, I hurt for her. For the woman she is, and for the woman I once knew who did the same thing.

She fought too. She fought and she lost.

It's so easy to hide behind anger, but it gets you nowhere. I can help her though. I need this too. The very thought of what I could do for her makes my blood ring with desire.

"I hate you!" Bethany's words are barely heard through the speaker, seeing as how I've turned them down so low.

In an attempt to ignore the thoughts and where they're headed, I check my phone and notice a flurry of texts, coming one after the other.

I text my brother, Carter, back without reading much of what he wrote. *I'm busy. Can we talk tonight?*

His response is immediate. *We need to talk about how we're going to deal with this situation.*

This situation … meaning Romano. The next name on a list of men I'll put ten feet in the ground.

A grunt barely makes its way through my clenched teeth as I write him back. *Push him out of his window, his own property.*

Let his body fall onto the spiked fence surrounding his estate.

Make an example of him.

I keep messaging him as the thoughts come, one line after the other.

Carter's answer doesn't come for longer than I'd like. My gaze is drawn again to Bethany, lying exhausted on the floor, and covering her face to hide the pain.

Fuck. I don't know how the hell it came to this.

Finally, he answers. *It's not that easy. There are complications.*

I stare at my phone, but my attention is brought back to the security monitors when Bethany finally stands, making her way to the bed. She stares at the door for a long time, sitting cross-legged and tense.

Jase, we need to wait for this one.

I don't have time for complications. I don't have patience for this. I don't have a desire for any of this. He should be dead already.

I turn off the phone, unwilling to spend another second dealing with this shit.

I want to get lost and find myself somewhere else.

Glancing at the screen, I watch Bethany pull a book into her lap. She must've gotten it from her purse. I went through the contents of her bag before I retrieved her from the trunk. Everything's there, except for her keys and a pen. I've seen both used in more violent ways than one could imagine.

She brushes the hair away from her face, showing me her vulnerability as she closes her eyes, and calms herself down.

I can get lost in her.

I lock the door to my office as I make my way to her, letting the keys clink against one another. My thumb runs along the jagged teeth of the key to the guest room as I think about stealing the fight from her, dragging it out of her and giving her so much more.

I'm careful with the lock, even more careful as I silently push open the door to her room. I don't stop at a crack, I keep pushing until the door is wide open and I can easily step through the threshold. It's quiet, so quiet in fact, that at first I don't see her.

Her small form is still on the bed, and only the sound of a page turning alerts me to where she is. With the overturned dresser, splintered wood and ripped curtains, she could have been hiding anywhere in here.

She ripped out every drawer. She threw two across the room, denting the drywall and cracking the walnut furniture.

Fragments of wood litter a corner of the room where she demolished a drawer, slamming it on top of another.

What a waste of energy. She should've saved it for this moment.

Instead the poor girl is still, curled up in a ball, and has her nose buried in the book.

She still doesn't see me, not even as I take a step forward, carefully stepping over a broken drawer.

The empty dresser, thick damask curtains and neatly made bed with bright white linens were all that were in the room. And now the fabric is heaped on the floor, the curtains ripped from the oil-rubbed bronze finishings and the armoire is … wrecked.

And little Miss Bethany sits in the middle of the bed, worn out and oblivious.

Her hair's a chaotic halo around her shoulders. The faint light from the setting sun casts a shadow around her, but it highlights her hair and when she tucks a strand behind her ear, it hits her face. Her fair skin's so smooth, it tempts me to brush my fingertips against it. The light falls to the dip in her neck, to the hollow there and it dares me to kiss her in that spot.

My cock hardens as I wonder what sounds would spill from her lips if I were to do just that.

"Looks like you had some fun." My voice comes out harder than I anticipated, startling her. She practically screams and slams her book shut as her body jostles.

She stands abruptly, backing off of the bed and clutching the book to her side as she squares her shoulders. "Let me go."

The huff comes back to me, but this time it's with a hint of humor.

"You're good at making demands when you have no authority, aren't you?" I question her, feeling a smirk play at my lips.

Silence. It's so fucking silent in this room, I think I can hear her heart pounding.

"Did you think destroying your room would … upset me?" I ask her with a deliberate casual tone to my question. Rounding the bed, moving closer to her, I kick a scrap of broken wood away from me. I follow her gaze as she glances at it, and then to the chunk of wood she left on the bed where she was sitting.

"Leave it there." I give her the command and watch her resist the urge to lunge toward it.

Her plump lips tug into a feigned smile. It's faint, but it's there. She is a fighter. There's no denying that.

"Did you want to anger me, Bethany?"

She flinches every time I say her name. That hint of a smile vanishes and the smoldering hate returns.

"I don't care what you do with this room. I won't be cleaning it up." I shrug as I add, "I hope it calmed you down to make such a mess."

With a gentle shake of her head, she huffs a humorless laugh at me then says, "Whatever you do to me, know that it won't hurt me. Whatever it is, I'll give you nothing."

She practically sneers her words, even as her eyes gloss over.

"We need to come to an agreement, and seeing as how you've gotten some of your… displaced anger out of the way-"

"Fuck you. I'm not agreeing on a damn thing with--"

"Not even to get the hell out of here?" I ask and cut her off.

The anger wanes from a boil to a simmer as her glare softens. "Just like that?" she asks skeptically.

"I don't want to keep you locked up… breaking all my shit." I make a point of kicking a piece of broken wood to the side. "I didn't plan this. And I want something else."

"So you're going to just let me go?"

"Once we come to an agreement, that's exactly what I plan on doing."

Shock lights her eyes, but so does skepticism.

"Do you think you can be reasonable this time?" I ask her, feeling I have the upper hand via the element of surprise.

"You fucking kidnapped me," she scoffs, the control leaving her in an instant. I watch as her knuckles turn white from how she grips the book so damn hard.

I take another stride forward to the end of the bed, and now only a few feet and a puddle of cotton linens stands between us.

Bethany takes a half step back, but when she tries to take another, her heel hits the balled-up curtain on the floor behind her. The wall is next.

"You tried to shoot me." My words cut through the air, leaving no room for negotiation as I add, "You should be dead for trying something so stupid."

At my last word, she steps behind the bundle of fabric at her feet, pressing her back to the wall. Her body trembles even as she utters the words, "Fuck you."

"I'm sure a well-read woman such as yourself has a wider vocabulary to choose from," I taunt and then nod to the book in her hand. "What is it?"

She breathes in and out, staring at me and refusing to speak.

"What book are you reading?" I ask her with less patience.

"I don't know," she answers, not taking her eyes from me.

"Now you're deliberately pissing me off," I tell her without any attempt at hiding the irritation.

"I don't know," she repeats, raising her voice, and her words come out hoarse. All that screaming she did caused more harm than good.

"Bullshit," I grit out and reach for the book, pissed off that she's being so stubborn, so resistant. With a single lunge forward, I grip the book in my hand, the other finding her hip to pin her against the wall.

"No!" she screams out at me, ripping the book away, and the thin pages on top nearly rip off without the cover to shield them. She turns her small body away from me as I press my chest against her. Barely managing to turn herself to face the wall, she cradles the book against her chest with both hands, concealing it from me. "It's my sister's." Her words are more of a cry than anything else, but the tone of them holds her explanation. "It's the last thing she gave to me," she bellows against the wall.

"I just got it yesterday; I don't know what book it is." Her voice lowers as her shoulders shudder. "There's no cover and I don't know what it is."

So this is what it takes to make her cower? An attempt to steal a book from her?

She's a trapped, scared, wild creature with nowhere to run and not sure how to fight, holding on to defiance because she has nothing else. I see her so clearly.

One breath, and then another. I stand there and just let her breathe.

"I believe you. Calm down."

"Calm down?" she shrieks at me, her voice wavering.

"Lower your voice or you'll stay in this fucking room

until I feel like letting you out." I practically hiss the low threat, backing away slightly, but still remain close enough that she doesn't turn around. "Let me see it," I demand, holding out my hand. "I'll give it back."

She's still and quiet for a long moment as my hand hovers in the air.

"There are times to fight and times to give in," I say calmly and then add, "I might know what book it is."

Thump. My heart pounds in my chest as she still doesn't react. Hope starts to wane, but before I have to decide what to do with her, she turns to face me, and hesitates only a second more before giving me the book.

"Do you read a lot?" she asks me as I skim the first page and then turn it over to examine the back.

Before I can reply, a small sigh of amusement erupts from her lips and then she covers her mouth. I can't help but to watch as her fingers trail down her lips before she lets her hand fall to her side. "Sorry," she says. "That's a ridiculous question."

"It's a ridiculous situation, so it's a fair question," I answer her evenly, letting her see how easy it could be if she just gives in.

Holding the book out to her, I shake my head and say, "I don't anymore, and I don't recognize it either."

Her fingers barely brush against mine as she takes the book back, and the heat in her touch is electrifying. So magnetic, I nearly slip my hand forward, desperate for more. Her lashes flutter as she moves away from me, pulling back as much she can and wrapping her arms around herself. "What do you want from me?"

The immediate response is disappointment, and

something else. There's a twisting feeling inside that feels like a loss, but I would have had to have possession of her in the first place to justify this feeling deep in the pit of my stomach.

"I have an offer for you and then I'll let you go," I tell her simply, acutely aware of the way each word sounds controlled.

"Is that a promise?" she asks as her gaze lifts to mine and she shakes her head in disbelief.

"Only because you'll be coming back."

In return she bites her bottom lip, effectively silencing herself, but the rage is clearly written on her face.

"You want to hate me." I address her anger before anything else.

"Yes," she answers quickly and honestly.

"That's only going to hurt you." The rawness in my words comes from a place I don't recognize.

She answers me, but she chokes up as she says, "I'm fine with that."

The twisting in my gut gets sharper. The seconds pass, and the air changes subtly between us, each of us staring at the other and waiting for the next move.

"What do you know about Marcus?" I ask her pointedly.

She shrugs like none of this matters, as if she isn't breaking apart. "I heard my sister say his name. He had something for her."

"What else?" I push her for more.

"Nothing." She looks me in the eyes and says, "All I had was his name and yours when she left."

"Nothing else?" I finally ask her when I judge her

response to be sincere. "Nothing about the drugs?"

"You're all drug dealers," she bites back.

"Now Marcus is a drug dealer?"

"He must be. Just like you must be."

"Why do you say that?"

"Because my sister bothered to learn your name."

"What name is that?"

"Cross."

"So when you said you know all about Marcus and the drugs…"

"I wanted to …" She can't finish. Her lips press into a thin line before she finally says, "I wanted it to sound like I had you."

Time moves quickly as I stare at her and she stares back.

"I wanted you to feel like you weren't going to get away with it," she whispers, breaking the silence and rubbing her arms.

"That's all you know?"

"One of you had her killed." She croaks the quick response and I can see the frustration on her face from not being able to keep it together.

"It wasn't me or anyone who works for me," I tell her calmly, keeping my voice low and steady and looking her in the eyes just like she did me.

When she doesn't react, I add, "You have questions; I can give you answers."

"What happened to my sister?" she asks me without allowing a second to pass.

"I don't know exactly, but I can find out. And more importantly, it's not going to happen like this. I have a way of doing things and a desire to handle things in a certain manner."

She stares at me like I'm the devil and she's searching for a way to escape. There's no escaping from this though.

"You'll get the answers you want and pay off the debt your sister owed."

"What do you get?"

"It will be tit for tat. I seem to remember you mentioning Marcus and something else about drugs?" I press and she blanches. "But I like things done a certain way. When I have questions to ask and I need to make sure the person giving me an answer is telling the truth."

"What way is that?" she asks in a single breath. The nerves are making her shoulders shake slightly.

There's no way I can tell her; I have to show her instead.

"Every ten minutes is a hundred dollars." I make up the amount on the spot and before I can calculate anything else, she questions, "Ten minutes of what?" She doesn't bother to hide the trepidation in her voice.

I can see her nervousness, the anger barely hidden.

"I'm not going to lie, Bethany. One of the reasons I didn't kill you where you stood in your foyer is because I find you…" I trail off as I debate on the next words I want to say, but take a risk.

"I think you're beautiful and I love the way you fight me."

Her lips part, her breathing coming in short gasps, and her chest flushes with a subtle blush that trails up her neck. The compliment leaves her more amenable. Her eyes widen, the depths of the darkness taking over as what I want sinks in.

"And what do you expect me to do?" she asks and her words are rushed as if she doesn't already know.

"You'll see."

"I'm not a whore." Her barb is immediate and raw. "I don't care what my sister owed you." She lowers her voice to add, "I don't owe you anything."

A smirk tugs at my lips and I lean forward, letting my palm rest against the drywall just above her right shoulder. Bringing my lips to her ear, I tell her, "I don't have to buy sex and if and when we do fuck, it will be because you're begging me to be inside of you."

"Fuck you."

"Those words again." I tsk and then add, "You do owe me."

"I don't owe you shit. The person who killed my sister owes you, not me."

With her raised voice, the tension rises as well until I tell her, "Three hundred thousand dollars."

"I don't… my sister…" She struggles to finish her sentence, choking on her words, letting the number hit her. *Three hundred thousand dollars.*

That's more than she'll make in five years of working her ass off at the mental health hospital. I know what she makes, and every cent she has to her name was in the file Seth gave me.

I can see the way number piles on top of her; the very idea that she would have to pay that amount suffocates her. Stealing the life from her for only a moment before she tries to back away from me, but there's only the wall behind her. Nothing more, and nowhere to go.

"You have no choice."

"Jenny couldn't have..." It's not the debt that causes grief to settle in the depths of her eyes, it's the very idea that her sister owed that much money to men like my brothers and me.

"You have questions and want answers. I want my bar to be free of your bullshit." Although my words are harsh, my voice is calm, as soothing as it can be given the situation.

Her gaze whips up to mine, and she battles the need to hold on to the anger as my eyes roam down her body. The sleeve of her shirt is ripped, probably from her own doing. Her nails are chipped—again, probably from the way she's struggled in all of this and then destroyed everything she could get her hands on.

"You have aggression and you need a release; I can give you that."

She breathes a little heavier then says, "I want to leave."

"I want an answer."

Silence.

"You have a debt, an inherited debt and I'm giving you a way to pay it, free and clear."

"I don't owe you shit," she whispers, her pain laced in between each word, woven in the air between us. But more than that... I can hear the consideration evident by the lack of her animosity.

"It's your house, Thirty-four Holley Drive? Your sister was on your deed, wasn't she? I'm guessing she helped you get the loan before she fell down the path that took her away from you?"

I'm an asshole, a prick. I'm going to fucking hell for this. With every second that passes, Bethany struggles more and more to fight, because she can barely hold herself together. "She used your home as a marker for this loan. It's going to be paid."

It's cruel how I stand here, watching these words strike Bethany over and over. Each time taking a larger piece of her sister's memory and changing it. Changing how she remembered her. And how she feels about her now.

I am the devil she thought I was.

"It's not about the money for you though."

My statement brings her gaze to me as I add, "And I'm not interested in taking from you what you don't want to give."

Her lips part, bringing me closer to getting what I want.

"You want to do it, Bethany. You will do this. The curiosity will win out. And if you don't go through me, if you go back to pounding down doors and calling the police…" I let the unspoken threat dangle in front of her, allowing her to come to her own conclusion. "I'm a powerful man, but even I can't save someone from themselves."

My words seem to strike a chord with her, stealing what's left of her composure.

"I just want- "

I cut her off and say, "I can give you what you want. And you can give me what I want too. Or you can pay me three hundred thousand by the due date, which is in… eleven days." I make up a date, and then regret the fact that I didn't say tomorrow.

CHAPTER
8

Bethany

I DON'T KNOW HOW LONG I'VE SAT HERE, wondering why he let me go. I know I should be dead after what I did. He's a criminal, and he could have done whatever he wanted with me. Before or after I shot that gun. He's strong enough to, and he has the means to do it. I've learned that much.

The sun's gone down, leaving my small living room bathed in shadows. My eyes burn, and my left ankle is numb from sitting on it for so long.

There's a bus that runs from the next block over all the way to Jersey City. I've been thinking about that too. And whether or not I would be able to use my credit cards, or if he'd be able to track me. I don't have enough cash to live without cards. I barely have any cash, in fact. There's a lot of debt in my name if I were to run and somehow try to

WWINTERS

come up with a fake ID.

I guess I can add three hundred thousand more to that debt. My stomach sinks at the thought, somehow finding its way to my throat even though it's in the opposite direction.

I've been waiting for some miraculous plan to smack me in the face. An easy way out, or even a difficult one. Something tells me Jase Cross will find me though. He'll find me wherever I run.

I can hear my back crack as I slowly rise from the sofa. My body is so stiff and sore, an obvious reminder of what happened. I need to give in to sleep and rest, but I can't bring myself to do it. To go lie in my bed when I'm so fucked.

Three hundred thousand dollars. What did you get yourself into, Jenny?

I have nothing. No money saved, only debt from school and from bailing Jenny out countless times. No answers to what happened.

He has answers. The nagging voice reminds me of that fact as I walk around my coffee table, leaving the book where it sits, and heading to the kitchen.

He wants to use me and pressure me into this when I don't deserve this shit. And he's the one with all the power. The one with all the answers.

Answers that belong to me. If he wants that debt to be paid, he'd better hold up his end of the deal. He'd better give me answers.

Grabbing a glass from the dishwasher and one of the many open bottles of red wine from my fridge left by all my unwelcomed guests, I decide on a drink. A drink to numb it all.

It's what I relied on last night too, after hours of searching my sister's old room for anything at all. Drugs she could have bought, cash she stored somewhere. I have no fucking idea how she owes so much, but her room was barren.

When Jase Cross dropped me off and told me he'd be seeing me soon, that was the first thing I did. Then I searched everywhere else. I searched and dug until my body gave out. And then I drank, somehow finding a moment of sleep, only to wake up with a pounding headache and that sick feeling still in my gut.

The way he said he'd be seeing me soon, before unlocking the car doors and walking me to my front door, the way he said it was like a promise. Like a promise a long-lost lover makes.

Not at all like the threat it really is.

The cork pops when it comes out, that lovely sound filling the air, followed by the sweet smell of Cabernet.

One glass quiets the constant flood of questions and regrets.

Two glasses numb the fears and makes me feel... alive. Free? I don't know.

Three glasses and I usually give in and pass out and everything's better then. Until I wake up and have to face another day with nothing to take this emptiness inside of me away.

He has answers.

Jase fucking Cross.

Ever since he let me go, my wrists and throat have felt scarred with his touch, and his voice has lingered in the back of my thoughts.

I hate that he makes me feel so much. There's a spark between us I can't deny. He doesn't hide it, and that only makes this all hotter. It's in the way he talks to me, his candor and tone. The way his gaze seems to see through me while also seeing all of me, every bare piece of me. There is nothing that isn't raw in the tension that ties us together. Raw and thrilling... and terrifying.

I shouldn't find the arrogant prick so hot. He's a criminal and an asshole.

It doesn't matter if I want to fuck him. I still hate him. I hate what he does to earn a living and what he stands for. I hate that in her last months, he may have seen my sister more than I did.

Hate doesn't do what I feel toward him justice.

He has to know there's no way I can pay him three hundred thousand dollars.

He has to know and that's why he's given me this "out" – it's coercion at best. I could take him to court, but I already went to the cops. And going to them got me nothing. Not a damn thing but Jase fucking Cross knocking at my door.

"I don't trust him," I whisper to no one, letting my fingertip drag along the edge of the wine glass before tipping it back, gulping down the chilled liquid. "I don't trust anyone anymore."

I almost called the cops. The very second I shut the front door after saying goodbye as if he was an old friend, not a bad man wrapped in a good suit, and pushed my back against it. I almost did it and then I remembered doing the same damn thing yesterday, and the day before and the day before that. No one can help me.

Jase has answers. The voice doesn't shut up. I slam the glass down hard on the counter. Too hard for being this sober. Barely caring that the glass isn't broken, I grab the bottle and pour the rest of it into the glass. It's more than enough to help me pass out and to leave me with a hangover in the morning.

With both of my hands on the counter, I lean forward, stretching and going over every possibility.

If I stay, he's either going to try to fuck me or kill me. And I must be insane, because I think it's all worth it if I get answers.

I'm willing to risk it just to feel something else – something other than this debilitating pain. "I've lost my fucking mind."

Just as the words leave me, I hear a ping from the living room and turn my head to stare down the narrow walkway of my kitchen.

My gaze moves from the threshold, to the fridge and I purse my lips before making my way to where the other bottles are hiding from me.

My bare feet pad on the floor and it's the only sound I hear as I grab the next partially drunk bottle from the fridge, the glass from the counter, and move back to where my ass has made an indent in the sofa.

Pulling the blanket over my lap, I sit cross-legged and read the text. I'm trying to prepare myself for any number of things. The trepidation, the anxiety, both are ever constant, but dampened with yet another sip of the sweet wine.

It's only Laura, though. Seeing her name brings a small

bit of relief until I read what she wrote.

Where the hell are you?

Home. What's wrong?

I went there yesterday. What happened to your door?

That sick feeling creeps up from the pit of my stomach and rises higher and higher until I'm forced to swallow it down with another gulp. This wine is colder, and it gives me a chill when I drink it.

Lie.

Just lie.

I know I should. I need to. I won't bring her into this bullshit. It's my problem, not hers.

You know I'm Italian, I answer her. Hoping the bit of humor mocking my hot-tempered heritage will lighten her mood.

You broke your door?

Italian and Irish, can't help it. Even I smirk at my answer. My mom used to tell us we're mutts, a mix of Italian and Irish, so people should know we'll hit them first if they're coming for us, and we won't stop hitting until we hit the floor. She was a firecracker, my mom.

The memory of her, of us, stirs up a sadness I keep at bay by filling my glass again. Three glasses, in what, twenty minutes? Even I can admit that's too much.

What happened? Laura asks.

Staring at the full glass, but not taking a sip, I settle with a half-truth. *My boss told me I have to take time off.*

Is it paid?

I get a little choked up thinking about how everyone chipped in to donate their PTO and debate on telling her the details, but hell, I can't deal with all this shit right now.

I've never felt so overwhelmed in every way in my entire life. So I keep it simple.

Yeah. It's paid.

I miss you, she writes back. Thankfully, not continuing a subject that's going to push me over the edge.

I'm teetering on the wrong side of tipsy, exhausted, mourning, angry and in denial of fear and loneliness. And being coerced into … probably sex, by a man I thought was going to kill me.

Fuck any kind of therapeutic conversation right now. Whether it's with Laura or anyone else. I don't have the emotional energy for it.

I miss you too.

We should go drunk shopping next weekend. Laura's suggestion sounds like a good way to have a minor public breakdown and max out my credit card. Which is fine if I do decide to leave town on the bus to Jersey City.

We can start at the mall, hit the restaurant bars in between the department stores? she suggests. The best times I've had with Laura were on the edge of a barstool holding a bag in one hand and a drink in the other, all while laughing about old times.

Hell yes, I answer her, because that's how I always answer her. Whether I'm going or not, I'll let her think I am so she feels better.

I promised I'd make you go out, so boom. Look at me keeping my commitment. I can practically hear the laughter in her voice from that text.

Who would have thought drunk shopping was a commitment you could keep, I joke back.

Seriously though, we haven't talked. How are you? Do

you need me to come over? Laura's message makes me pause. But I can't hesitate for too long. She's sent me that message before, *do you need me to come over*, when in reality she was five minutes away and already headed here. She's notorious for just dropping in on people like that and thinks it's cute. In all honesty, I'm glad she's done it in the past, but I can't tonight. I will break down and tell her everything.

Don't come, I'm fine. I think I needed the time off, I admit to Laura after writing several messages and deleting them all.

If she came over… it would be disastrous.

Life moves too fast. It's whirling around me, demanding, taking, and I don't even have time to do an inventory of what's left of me. I don't know how to be okay, and I want someone to hurt for what happened to Jenny. I want someone who deserves it to be in this pain.

Someone other than me. It's so easy to blame myself. I deserve some of it. I can admit it.

I don't tell Laura any of that though. A small part of me knows she already knows I blame myself. No matter how many times she's told me you can't help someone who won't help themselves. It doesn't change the fact that Jenny was my sister. It doesn't change the fact that I keep thinking if only I'd been with her, or if I'd followed her, if I'd pushed her more, maybe she'd still be with me.

I don't even realize I'm crying until I feel the tears on my cheeks.

Angrily, I wipe them away and toss my phone across the coffee table. It makes the glass clatter against the table as I cover my face with my hand and force myself to calm down.

I just need to know what happened. I need to know.

Jase Cross will get me answers.

The very thought has my eyes opening, and the need to mourn subsiding.

My gaze wanders to the foyer. To the small table that sits right where it should, but was pushed to the side only hours ago. To the wall he pushed me against. The scene plays out in my head, complete with the bang of a gun and his husky voice whispering against the shell of my ear.

As I remember his words, shivers run down my shoulders. I'll blame some of them on the wine.

He may not have hurt her, but he knows who did, or he knows someone who can find out. He knows *something* about the side of my sister I never fully knew.

I want it. I need it. I need to know.

As my phone pings with another text, there's a knock at my door.

Fucking Laura. I love her, but I cannot deal with life right now. I don't bother picking up the phone to see what she wrote this time.

Instead I'm focused on one glaring thought that won't leave me alone as I stand up. I know nothing about the world my sister inhabited. I know nothing about the life she led.

All I know is this, my work, my small circle, and the daily patterns that haven't changed in years.

But Jase Cross knows it all.

Making my way to the door, I come up with every excuse I can to make her go away; looking down past my baggy pajama shirt all the way to the stains on my old sweatpants, my very appearance is excuse enough. I need to pass the hell out and be alone.

I'm already telling her to go home when I open the door, wide and easily, not even considering for a second that it isn't her.

"You aren't touching my wine-" I start to joke with her, but then my jaw drops open and my heart stutters. My body heats with both fear and desire, making my grip on the doorknob slip as Jase stares down at me.

He's taller than I remember; how is that even possible? His shoulders are wide and dominating as he stands in my doorway. A ribbed black Henley under a thick wool coat and dark jeans are all he wears this time. For some reason, comparing the two sides of him, this casual man with an edge of seduction and the buttoned-up powerful man of control… it stirs a heat in my core.

"What do you want?" My words are rushed and I try desperately to hold on to what little sense I have.

"You look surprised." His voice is smooth like velvet, caressing every one of my senses.

"What are you doing here?" I question him, feeling panic rise inside of me.

With a sexy smirk kicking up his lips, he runs the pad of his thumb down the sharp line of his jaw before telling me, "I'm here with your contract."

CHAPTER
9

Jase

S HE'S LESS THAN SOBER. THE WINESTAINED LIPS
tell me that.
She hasn't slept, judging by her messy hair and
the darkness under her eyes.

And I can tell by the response of her body when she
looks into my eyes that she needs to be fucked. Hard and
ruthlessly. Fucked into her mattress until she can't do anything but sleep away everything that plagues her.

Good fucking timing for me. I've never given in to
these desires. It's only been a fantasy. I know she's hurting
and so am I. There is a certain kind of pleasure that can
soothe such a deep pain. I fucking need it. Right now.

The thoughts run wild in my head as I wait for her to
let me in.

The foyer is just how I remembered it. A classic '50s

house with a mix of modern and antique furniture that give it a comfortable feel. She's eclectic. Or at least her belongings are.

The chill of the winter air moves with me as I take a long stride inside, forcing Bethany to take a step back. Her stride is shorter though and she bumps her ass into the hall table, turning around as she startles, and I take the moment to close the door.

"I didn't say you could come in." She breathes out her words and stumbles at finding her anger and her strength to keep me away. I almost feel bad catching her off guard. But then again, that's how she caught me yesterday.

"We got off on the wrong foot." I ignore her statement, taking a step toward her but making sure to be as non-threatening as I can. With my hands slipping into my front pockets I meet her questioning gaze, and each passing moment it heats with an anger she's barely concealing.

"I apologize," I offer, seeing that fight come and go inside of her. She has no idea what to do, and my apology gives her whiplash.

Her lips part, but no words come out. Her hands move behind her, gripping the small table and I swear I can hear her heartbeat loud and clear. As if it's pounding inside of her just for me.

Still no words have come but her lips stay parted, and her gaze remains questioning.

"I shouldn't have come in here like I did, making demands. I think we can come to terms in a civilized manner."

A crease mars her forehead as Bethany brushes the hair from her cheek and tucks it behind her ear.

"You're a criminal," she speaks lowly to the floor, but

her eyes rise to mine as she adds, "You think you can force your way into getting what you want and if that doesn't work, charm will?" Although she poses the statement as a question, I know she believes what she said wholeheartedly.

She's not wrong, but I won't give her that satisfaction.

"I've never been called charming, Bethany," I tell her, playing with the way I say her name. Softening it, letting it fall from my lips gently, as if simply whispering it allows it to hang in the air, hinting at all the things we're leaving unspoken.

It takes her a moment to say anything at all. The force in her words is absent, and she doesn't look me in the eyes.

"Apology accepted, please leave."

"We have unfinished business." My response is immediate.

I watch as she swallows, hating me but knowing I push more boundaries than just anger.

"I stand by what I said, you owe a debt." Her gaze snaps to mine and her exhale is forceful. I continue before she can object. "I wrote up a contract I think you'll find agreeable."

She's silent as I pull out the folded paper from my back pocket, along with the pen I lifted from her purse.

Her gaze narrows as she recognizes it. "You'll need to sit down for this. Standing in the hallway isn't how I conduct business."

Silence.

Ever defiant.

I fucking love it. I relish standing here while she makes me wait, as if she could actually control what happens next. Our story is already written, and she knows it. She'll give in. She knows that too.

Without saying a word, she stalks to her living room, her arms crossed over her chest until she sits.

Although I haven't been in the living room, I've already seen it. And the kitchen and dining room. I'm prepared for what's in every drawer. Seth took care of that for me.

There's a heavily poured glass of wine on the table, and she pours it back into the bottle rather than downing it like I thought she was going to do when she grabbed it.

"You can sit wherever you want, intruder."

"Intruder?" I question her and the only acknowledgement I get is a firm, singular nod in time with the glass being placed gently on the coffee table.

"All right then, *attempted murderer*," I quip back and take a seat on the armchair beside the sofa.

Her mouth drops open and then slams shut, her jaw tense as she stares back at me as if I've said something offensive. "Just calling a spade a spade," I say and hold her gaze as I raise my hands, palms toward her in defense.

She hesitates to respond and I know I see remorse in her eyes. I know what it looks like; I see it every fucking day.

"I would have done the same, just so you know," I confide in her and her tense shoulders ease a bit. Only a fraction though. "I don't blame you."

She's still silent for a moment, assessing me and everything she's dealing with.

I'll be gentle with her, I'll give her what she needs. I can be that man for her. And she can be what I need.

"What do you want?" she asks after a moment. "What contract?"

Leaning forward, I rest my elbows on my knees and lace my fingers together. "You have questions, needs, and so do I. You owe me a debt, whether you like it or not, and I can give you something you never knew you wanted."

Her thighs tighten as she swallows thickly, tensing her neck. She pulls the blanket closer to her and asks, "Did you know my sister?"

"Not personally, but I know things she was doing. She got into some trouble."

The reaction is immediate, her expression falling and for the first time I came in here, the pain shows, but she's quick to hide it.

"I'll answer your questions," she says softly, gaining control of her composure before looking at me and finishing her negotiation. "And you'll answer mine?"

A sorrowful smile plays at my lips. "That's not how this works." Her bottom lip wavers and her fingers dig into the comforter on her lap. "I want more."

The tension thickens between us with every passing second of silence.

The paper crinkles in my hand as I unfold it and read it to her.

"For the payment of three hundred thousand dollars, not a penny will be paid in currency. The party agrees that sessions will take place, in which Bethany Fawn allows Jase Cross to question her as he sees fit, questions she will answer honestly to the full extent of her knowledge, and in a manner that will entail no physical harm whatsoever to Miss Fawn. The ability for Bethany to stop all proceedings whenever she wishes, verbally, will halt the session, allowing Miss Fawn to leave as she wishes."

I watch her expression, noting how she squirms uncomfortably and pushes her hands into her lap and she then reads the last line.

"Every ten minutes is equivalent to one hundred dollars."

"That's thirty thousand minutes total, that's five hundred hours," Bethany says aloud with no indication in her tone as to what she makes of that sum.

"Correct."

"I couldn't possibly... that's a full-time job for a quarter of the year. I won't let this interfere with my job."

"It won't. We can add in a line if you'd like, stating that it will come second to your occupational needs."

"I would be in debt to you for a year at least."

"Yes," I say, and there's no negotiation in my tone.

"What about my questions?"

"They're yours to ask, but not a part of this contract."

"That's-"

I cut her off. "Not necessary to be included in a contract regarding how you'll be paying me back." I lean forward, holding her gaze. "I choose to answer your questions as a gesture of goodwill."

"And you'll continue to?" she pushes.

"I don't have a single problem answering every question you have. Tit for tat." She gives a small nod of acknowledgement, but nothing else.

Time passes and Bethany chooses not to push for that to be in writing.

"How will you be questioning me?" she asks and a warmth flows through me, the tension lighting slowly, crackling between us like a smoldering fire.

"Sign first," I answer, swallowing thickly as I pass the paper to her, followed by the pen. Her fingers brush against mine, gentle but hot. The sensation travels from my knuckle all the way up my arm, the nerve endings coming alive with heat.

My throat's dry and my blood hot just thinking about her allowing me to show her.

"You realize I'll never believe I owe you anything?" she questions me, a simple statement, so matter of fact.

"You owe me your life for that stupid shit you pulled. Whether you want to believe that or not."

She picks at some indiscernible fuzz on the blanket before whispering, "I'm sorry."

Remorse and conflict swirl in her gaze, but she's quick to hide it from me.

"I like that you're less angry."

"That happens when I greet the bottom of a green glass bottle with a label that reads Cabernet." Her tone is muted, but she gives a small huff of a laugh, and lets a smile kiss her lips for only a moment.

"I need to know what you're going to do to me," she says before clearing her throat. "I'm not naïve. I know ... I know you can do what you want. I know you may lie to me, hurt me, fuck me, whatever it is you intend to do, I'm not stupid." I can hear her swallow and then she adds, "But what if I did go along with it? Would you really tell me what happened to her?" Her eyes gloss over and her voice softens.

"A question for a question," I tell her. "An answer for an answer."

"You're going to be disappointed with my answers," she

says with a weary note to her voice. "She barely told me anything. I was speaking out of anger when I saw you."

"You came to my bar, you looked for my family. You tried to shoot me." With every sentence, she cowers more and more. "There's a reason for those actions." She nods solemnly.

"What are you going-"

"Just sign," I cut her off and she moves her focus to the empty glass. My pulse is racing, my nerves on edge. And yet, she looks so ... unaffected by the weight of what's to come. Like some part of her has given in.

"I need this as much as you do."

Her huff is nothing but sarcastic. Easy, I remind myself. Go easy on her now. It will be different later.

"It will be an escape from the pain if nothing else. You need it," I tell her and this time her expression changes slightly, as if she's so very aware of the agony that mourning is. It's also an aphrodisiac. There is never a more relevant time to be touched, or to be loved than when someone you love is gone.

"You want another glass?" I offer with a slight teasing tone to lighten the mood, an asymmetric grin pulling at my lips when she peeks up at me through her thick lashes.

"I may have had more than enough already."

The sofa groans as she leans back on it, reading the single sheet of paper once again.

The faint light from the disappearing sun kisses her skin as the loose shirt slips down her shoulder and she has to readjust it. She doesn't look back at me as she does. With her legs bent, her bare feet resting on the edge of the sofa and a thin blanket thrown over her lap, she looks far too casual for this moment.

As if that exposed skin of hers wasn't everything I've been thinking about since I first saw her across the bar. As if I don't want to rip that shirt off of her and devour every inch of her body with open-mouth kisses, dragging my teeth along her skin and making her that much more sensitive for what I'm going to do to her.

There are moments in time, pauses in your reality, where you realize this instant will be a memory forever. Something that will never leave you. I'll remember this one forever.

I hope I never forget how the adrenaline is rushing through me, how eager I am. I want to remember it all. Every single detail.

I'll remember it, and I'll have to, because I'm going to lose her. She's not meant to be mine.

That doesn't mean I won't take her, though.

"If I say no?" she asks, her wide hazel eyes searching mine for something.

"It doesn't happen." There's no hesitation in my answer.

"If I say stop?"

"It stops."

"Why do it then? Why would you do this?" she asks with her brow furrowed.

"Because I know you want it. I know you need it." She's silent in return.

"This would never hold up in court," she says, finally breaking the quiet.

"I have no desire to ever see you in a courtroom, Miss Fawn. I didn't even intend to write this down; I only did it because I thought you would respond better, maybe even listen to what I'm offering, if it was written in black and white."

"And what is it you're offering exactly, Mr. Cross?"

"Answers, and an escape, a way to pay a debt I know you can't afford." My gaze stays on hers, holding her in place until she gives me an answer. "This is a world you know nothing about, Bethany, and I'm willing to bring you into it. I'm willing... and you'd be wise to take this deal."

"Call me Beth." She corrects me without looking at me as the pen scribbles her signature, right on the line next to mine.

Desire sinks into my blood in an instant, surging through every fiber of my being as the paper and pen find themselves on the coffee table. Signed on the dotted line.

"I'll go easy on you," I tell her as I stand up, preparing myself to show restraint. She stays where she is, pretending not to be affected in the least.

"Is that right?" she asks as I pour a glass of wine. She stares at the dark liquid swirling before speaking out loud. "I'm already a little further than the right side of tipsy, Mr. Cross."

I fucking love the way she said my name. My cock stiffens, immediately hard just from having her obey me, having her speak to me like this. There's something about a fiery woman submitting that makes me lose all control and focus, giving it all to her.

"It's for me," I point out and take a sip. It's cheap wine, but decent enough.

"Don't confuse me going along with this for something it isn't," she says a little harder, with more resolve than I expect.

"Oh, and what isn't it?"

"I'm not just going to let you do what you want and get away with it. I'm not that easy, and I'm not submitting to your every wish if that's what you think this is."

A beat passes before I ask her, "Then what are you doing?"

"I'm simply learning the ropes of your world, Mr. Cross."

"This is how you'll learn. You'll do what I say. I ask the first question, then once I'm satisfied with your answer, you can ask me whatever you want. Those are the ropes, Miss Fawn."

Her long brown hair brushes against her shoulders as she nods, making her shirt fall once again and a shiver run across her skin. She's quick to lift the thin fabric back into place, as if it will be staying there.

"Lie down." I give her the first command and just like yesterday, in the guest bedroom when I waited for the book she held so tightly, she hesitates, testing me before obeying.

"I'd like to address an important matter first," she states innocently enough, arching a perfectly plucked brow at me.

"What's that?"

"It's seven seventeen," she tells me and I grin, letting the rush of desire take over.

"I already started the clock at six fifty-two when I pulled into your driveway."

Surprise widens her eyes.

"Lie down."

"I'll say no if you tell me to spread my legs for you."

The determination in her voice is surprising,

85

considering how badly she wants me.

Although I don't speak the sentiment out loud, I make her words a personal challenge.

"You'd spite me to deny yourself a basic need?" I ask her and before she can respond I add, "I have no intention of fucking you today, but I know you need to be fucked long and hard … both that mouth of yours and your cunt."

Indignation flashes in her eyes, darkening them, which only makes the golden hues that much more vibrant.

"If I put my hands between your thighs, would I find you hot and wet for me?" My voice is calm, although my dick leaks precum, throbbing from the very idea that her cunt is ready for me.

"You'll never know," she says offhandedly before lying down, covering herself with the blanket and resting her head on the one pillow that was tucked in the corner of the sofa.

"I asked you a question." My words are hard, and her hazel glare whips to mine. "Is your cunt soaking wet for me?"

"No." She answers savagely and begins to ask her own question, but I tell her, "I'm not satisfied with that answer."

I drop to my knees one by one to get closer to her, feeling her heat, but not touching her. Not yet.

Somehow I keep my voice low and controlled when I repeat my question, "Is your cunt soaking wet for me?" My breathing is short, my palms hot with desire raging inside of me.

Give in to what's to come, my cailín tine.

The Gaelic phrase fits her, everything about her, perfectly. My cailín tine. My fiery girl.

Lifting her head and staring boldly into my heated gaze, she answers, "You're an attractive man, Mr. Cross. I've been wet for you since you pinned me against my foyer wall." Her blink is slow and deliberate. When she opens her eyes, she stares at the ceiling as if her heart isn't racing out of her chest, as if the blush on her cheeks is only from the wine. With her hands on her chest, she gently places her head on the pillow and asks politely, "Is it my turn to ask a question?"

Sitting back, I rest my hands on the rustic wood floors on either side of my thighs, forcing myself not to touch her. It's so cold, and a much-needed reminder of how hot I burn for her.

"You aren't in the position I want yet, but yes, I did say I would go easy on you this first time."

"Who killed my sister?" Her words are blurted out and her body tenses. "I want a name," she adds quickly.

"I don't have a name, but I'm looking into it and when I do – which I will, I promise you – when I do have a name, I will tell you."

"So you're saying you had nothing to do with it?"

"That's another question, Miss Fawn. I'll gladly answer it now, but then I get two in a row."

Her wild eyes search mine for a moment as she clenches her jaw before nodding in agreement.

"Not only did I have nothing to do with her death, neither did my brothers or anyone who works for me. I have no idea why she was killed... yet."

She swallows thickly and her forehead scrunches as she wars with whether or not to believe me.

All I can think about is the one night at The Red Room.

I bet her sister told her about that night and that's why she came searching for me and knew to go to my club.

"Move your hands above you, to here," I say then reach up and pat the arm of the sofa. She's slow to obey, but she does. Her nails sink into the fabric and that loose shirt slips down her shoulder again, showing me more of her soft skin. I run a finger along the curve of her arm, leaving goosebumps along my path.

"I don't know-"

I cut off her objection. "I want to know when you're lying to me, and I'll do as I see fit." My words are barely spoken, because my focus is on how flushed her skin is already from such little contact.

I take my time, moving her hair to the side so I can see her slender neck and the dip in her collar.

Reaching into my left back pocket, I pull out a simple, black silk tie and tell her, "Your wrists will be bound." Her eyes flash to mine, and I take another sip of her wine. It's so much sweeter the second time, not unlike herself.

Although she watches as if she'd like to object, she doesn't. Instead all she says is, "Seven thirty-four."

"One thing you'll find benefits you greatly in this arrangement is that I enjoy taking my time," I tell her, picking up her left wrist, wrapping it and then the other before tying the two together. "Your body will tell me if you're lying to me. Your body will tell me *everything*."

All the while I watch her body. How her back arches slightly, how slowly she's blinking, how quickly she's breathing. I'm captivated by her and I couldn't give two shits if every word out of her mouth is a lie.

"You said you'd stop if I want you to?" she asks me and

I answer with a question of my own. "Are you already having doubts?"

"Just checking," she whispers as I tighten the knot and place her wrists back on the arm of the sofa, above her head. The nervousness colors her every move. She can't hide anything from me like this.

I don't ask her or warn her before I pull the blanket down, exposing her to the cool air, so at odds with her heat.

I'll go slow. I'll be gentle this first time and ease her into what I want.

Her hips dig into the sofa as if she's trying to get away or hide, before ultimately relaxing. Her thighs are pressed firmly together, all the way down her legs to her ankles, barely covered by the thin sweatpants. With her shirt pulled up from the way she's laying, there's a sliver of her midriff exposed.

"Let me tell you a secret." My fingers fall to just above the exposed skin, playing along the hem of her shirt and gently lifting it higher. "I often have to get answers from people. It's what I do; it's what I'm good at."

It's because of me that Carter was able to create this empire so quickly. Everyone had secrets and I was able to get them all. With a knife and ruthlessness he didn't have quite yet. Power is limited if you don't have the knowledge to enforce it.

Her body stiffens and the breath she releases is strained.

"When someone is put in a state where they can't control their body, their emotions," I say, watching her as she stares at the ceiling, waiting for her eyes to find mine before continuing, "their pain or their pleasure, they give so much away." I let my words linger in the air before my fingers finally fall to her exposed belly. I run the tips of my fingers just inside the waistband of her sweatpants. Just barely venturing lower. "I intend to tie you down, to push your limits, and to enjoy every detail you give me about whatever it is I want to know."

"I can say no," she gasps as I slip my hand lower, finding the elastic band of her underwear. The way her shoulders rise and hunch with every quick breath reveals her desire just as much as it displays her need to run.

"Of course you can, but why would you deny yourself if you have nothing to hide?"

"I don't have anything to hide."

"Prove it," I tell her.

"You just want to touch me." Her words fall carelessly from her lips.

"I want to do more than touch you," I admit to her and feel a pang in my chest. A longing that's desperate to be spoken. "You aren't the only one in this room who's in need."

At my words, her gaze drifts lower, down to my zipper and I'm sure she can tell how hard I am for her. Her mouth parts slightly and she looks away, not commenting but showing her cards all too easily.

My gaze wanders to the crook of her neck, and as she breathes, a lock of hair falls right where I'm looking.

Leaning forward, I brush it to the side and bring my lips closer to her ear. Intent on whispering, intent on sharing a part of me I haven't shared with anyone.

I want to run my lips along her neck, kissing and

sucking and confessing all my sins, begging for forgiveness.

Her chest heaves as if she knows I want to kiss her.

None of that happens though, because she turns her head just as I start to make my move, and she steals the kiss from me.

Her lips brush against mine at first, soft and hesitant. Yet she nips my bottom lip before I can deepen it. The gentleness of her touch is at odds with how my hands reach up to her hair, gripping it at the base of her neck and pulling her head back to expose more of her throat.

With my breath stolen, once again caught off guard, and with the desire running rampant in my blood, I stare down at her. Her eyes half lidded, her breaths coming in short pants as if I'd just devoured her and it wasn't at all a tempting taste of a kiss.

I'm drunk off her.

Breathing in her lust and not breaking her gaze, I lower my fingers to her swollen nub, spreading her arousal up to it, and then circling it. "What was that for?" I ask her and she tells me, "I wanted to take it first. I deserve that much at least." Her last word skips in the air, like a flat rock thrown across a summer lake. Her speech moves from a higher pitch to a whisper as I move my fingers lower, playing with her and watching every reaction she gives me.

"How many lovers have you had?" I ask and my question catches her off guard as she struggles to hold back her gasps.

"Few," she answers in a strained voice as I circle her clit again.

"Recently?"

"Not since college."

"Did they touch you like this?" I ask her, imagining a younger version of her under the sheets in a dorm room, letting some dumb fuck put his hands on her.

"Yes," she breathes with her eyes closed and I gently press down on her clit and then smack it.

She sits up and when she does I aim for another kiss, but she bites down hard on my mouth. Her teeth plunge into my bottom lip, the bite sending a pain shooting through my body. It's hard enough to draw blood and I swear to God it does nothing but make me that much harder for her.

She releases me all too soon, sucking in a deep breath with her mouth still open, her chest heaving and her eyes pinned on me.

Lifting my fingers from her heat, I bring them to my throbbing lip.

"No blood," she murmurs and a soft smirk plays on that pouty mouth of hers. "Don't get the wrong idea, Mr. Cross. Even if the thought of you getting me off makes me all hot and bothered, I still hate your fucking guts."

My dick responds, getting harder by the second as she utters the threatening words so sensually, words that would get others killed.

Her anger's at war with her desire, but it's losing the battle. Maybe it's the wine, maybe it's the exhaustion, but I can give her desire the upper hand.

I watch her every move. The way she clenches her hands and struggles to keep them motionless above her head. The way her skin flushes and goosebumps run up her chest, then down her arms. She's fucking gorgeous like this. Bared to me without reluctance. Without a single hint suggesting she's hiding a damn thing.

She's lost in the lust.

I spread her arousal around her swollen nub before bringing my middle finger back to her opening. With a gentle press, her lips part, and the word *stop* is there, just behind her clenched teeth. The hiss of an S was coming.

I push her, barely sliding the tip of my finger into her hot entrance, and her jaw drops open, the word lost somewhere and remaining unspoken.

Bringing my fingers back to her clit, I let her come down from the high, simply toying with her as she regains her composure.

"That's your limit?" I ask her, bringing my fingers back up to her clit, watching as her eyes go half lidded and she exhales with pleasure. My fingers drift back down and press against her slick entrance slightly before she nods a yes to my question.

Her control is as surprising as my restraint. If I hadn't decided I wasn't going to fuck her tonight, not until she truly begs for it, she'd be screaming my name as I ravaged her on the carpet beneath me. Maybe bent over the coffee table to leave bruises on her hips as a reminder. Making sure she'd feel it tomorrow, so it would be all she could think about.

I need to be gentle today. I'll ease her in until she's drowning in the pleasure I'm so desperate to give her.

She can barely breathe. Her gasps and held breaths are making her body tremble just as much as my touches are.

"Cum." My singular word bites through the air as I land a hard smack on her clit and then capture her scream of pleasure with my own kiss. My kiss is more ruthless than hers as I let my tongue delve into her hot mouth. It's quick like hers though; I pull back both the kiss and my touch, just as soon as it began.

She can barely keep herself still, her body begging her to move away from the sensation, but she needs more. Pulling her shirt down, I move her bra so it pushes her breast up, and before she can object I lean forward and swirl my tongue around her nipple. Her thighs move together and stagger to the side.

Still sucking on her, I smack her thigh with the back of my hand, pushing her legs open and moving my hand to cup her pussy.

Letting her nipple out of my mouth with a pop, I pull back to tell her, "Your cunt is soaking wet for me," and rub ruthless circles around her clit, making her brow pinch, her mouth open and her body shudder with another climax.

Her entire body spasms with the second orgasm. And I can barely fucking stand to watch with how hard I am. Everything in me begs me to shove my cock down her throat.

Still panting and struggling, Bethany lets her hands fall forward and then quickly moves them back into place on the arm of the sofa. Her eyes search mine for direction with a desperate apology to forgive her swimming in their darkness.

In answer, I pull the tie loose. She came, she let me touch her. I need to get the hell out of here before I fuck her and ruin it all before it's even begun.

"Next time will be more intense. You should prepare yourself."

Her first words as I reach for the contract, still on the table, bring a genuine smirk to my lips. "You didn't ask your question."

"I know."

It's quiet for a moment as I tuck the contract into my back pocket.

"Why are you doing this?" Her bright eyes are wide and full of fire. Full of an intense desire and a curiosity that are addictive. Every look she gives me brings out more life, more heat, more passion in me to coax more of this from her. She burns like wildfire and I want to add fuel to her flame.

"I wanted you to see why I let you live. What I wanted from you against that foyer wall after you pulled that trigger." Although her chest rises and falls rapidly, the memory of yesterday adding fear into the cocktail of emotions she's drunk on, the golden flecks in her hazel eyes stay lit. Her lips part slightly, and I know the memory only gets her off just like it does to me.

"It was an accident," she admits to me.

My smirk widens into an asymmetric grin. "Is that supposed to make me feel better about it?" I ask her and she simply shakes her head, pulling her shirt down and reaching for the thin blanket to cover herself. Her skin is still flushed, the pleasure still rocking through her, but her eyes are focused on the digital clock below her television.

Ever a reminder.

My smile falls as I tell her, "You're reckless."

"You're the one who was almost murdered by someone like me. So who's really reckless?"

"Maybe I'm just reckless for you," I answer without

thinking, barely hearing my words before recognizing them.

I warn her, "Next time I won't ask for your boundaries."

"I would have--"

"Next time I'm going to fuck you like both of us want me to."

CHAPTER
10

Bethany

I FEEL LIKE I'M DROWNING. LIKE I'M IN OVER MY head, and I don't know how I ventured into the dark abyss of the ocean, sure to swallow me whole.

I dreamed of him. I dreamed of Jase fucking me, taking me ruthlessly on the sofa. I dreamed of telling him no, only to have him pin me down and take me regardless.

The thought sends a blush of desire to grace my skin, kissing it and leaving a shiver in its wake. The way Jase did last night. Every small touch brought more and more heat, more sensitivity, more life. I felt alive under him.

And I want more. I'm not ashamed to admit I want more of Jase Cross.

Bringing my fingertips to my lips, I remember the kiss I drunkenly stole—thank God I can blame it on the alcohol. He tasted like bad decisions and lust. A sin waiting to happen.

When did my life become like this?

Working every day has kept my thoughts at bay. And now I have nothing to occupy my time. Nothing but a debt to Jase Cross and unanswered questions I have no way of answering on my own.

The only thing I've been working on is looking up every detail I can on Jase Cross. Hardly anything comes up at all about any of his brothers. All I can tell is that they were a poor Irish family, raised in the hellhole that is Crescent Falls. Back then they were nothing. And now they're everything.

There are only four pictures of Jase that I could find. Two had the same woman in them. In one, she's in the background, laughing at something. It's a candid photo and it seems harmless enough. But in the second, her arm is around him. It was taken nearly five years ago, and Jase looks much younger.

I have no fucking clue who she is.

Although, she looks a little like me in this picture, the second one. Only slightly. But the resemblance spreads an eerie chill over my body when I think about it.

Is this who I remind him of?

Was he with her? The fact that I feel any hint of jealousy is ridiculous.

I haven't been touched since college, and I haven't wanted a damn thing from a man since that catastrophe.

Maybe I've always been jealous like this, and I just didn't know it because I had nothing to be jealous of. It only took the strike of a single match to ignite a blazing desire to overtake every piece of me.

Maybe this is what it was like for Jenny. One small change, and everything fell from there. Addiction is like that, isn't it? No matter what your addiction is.

The sound of my phone vibrating on the kitchen counter saves me from the downward spiral of my thoughts.

It's only Laura, checking in again since I didn't respond to her last night.

A few quick texts and I'm free of her prying questions, plus I've booked a date with a bottle of tequila, her, and the outlet mall next weekend.

The phone clatters on the kitchen counter when I toss it down, staring at it and wondering what that night will end up being. A few drinks, and I'll tell her the sordid details.

I know I will.

I can see it unfolding in front of me.

She won't judge me, seeing as how she's had a few one-night stands. She's gone backstage with an out-of-town band before, only to be seen again at 2 p.m. the next day, walking a little funny but smiling so hard that it didn't matter.

It's not the judgment that concerns me. I couldn't care less about what people think of me.

If Laura thinks I'm in danger though, she'll get involved. The very thought makes me let out a slow quivering breath, calming the rush of anxiousness.

I can't keep Jase my dirty little secret, but some things will have to be just that. A secret. I'll let him use me, and I'll use him. Every encounter with him is a step closer to the world my sister lived in before I lost her. It's closer to where she was and closer to finding out what happened. At least the thought is somewhat calming.

Knock, knock, knock.

Three raps in quick succession sound through the first floor of my house. I've never been so grateful for a distraction before.

Looking out through the peephole, I see a man in a gray wool coat, a man I don't recognize.

Maybe he has a package, or maybe he's a neighbor. I hesitate to open the door, my hand gripping the knob tight as I consider getting the gun. That didn't turn out well last time though, and I refuse to live in fear.

It's just a man. Not everyone is a villain.

The last thought firms my resolve and I pull open the door halfway, wincing when I feel the sharp coldness in the air.

"Hello," I greet him easily, immediately struck by how handsome he is.

Classically handsome with striking blue eyes and a charming smile. This man has definitely left broken hearts behind in his wake.

The small smile from the thought fades.

Nervousness pricks along the back of my neck. Every hair is standing on edge when I glance behind him, only to see a cop car.

He's a fucking cop.

"Ma'am, I'm Officer Cody Walsh," he tells me, taking off his gloves and reaching out his hand to shake mine.

Every ounce of me is consumed with fear, nausea, and the suspicion that this is a setup. I shake his hand without thinking, without considering a damn thing.

Even though he was wearing gloves, his strong hand is ice cold and I feel the chill flow from his touch straight to the marrow of my bones.

It's not until I swallow my nerves, nearly ten seconds after shaking his hand while he only stares at me curiously, that I'm able to speak.

"Could I see your badge?"

He's quick to take it out, passing it to me and when he does, his fingers brush against mine. The physical contact is a little too close I think at first, but then I peek up at him and he's all business. It's all in my head.

"Sorry, I just didn't expect to see any more cops now that the funeral's passed," I tell him, whipping up the excuse on a dime and praying it explains my hesitation as I pass back his badge. Again his fingers brush mine and although I'm well aware of that fact, he doesn't show any sign that he noticed.

"The funeral?" he questions and I feel the blood drain from my face.

"My sister's; isn't that why you're here?" My voice is calm but drenched in sorrow. Real sorrow. I stand there pretending I know nothing of the past few days but my grief. I think back to what I felt the night my estranged family left me alone and I had to sleep knowing Jenny was really gone. That the world has accepted that, and I needed to as well.

I'm only a sister in mourning. That's all I choose to be right now.

"I'm sorry to hear about your loss." He clears his throat, bringing his closed fist to his mouth as he looks to his right, away from me and then adds, "I'm here on different matters."

Finally, he looks back at me, and at the same time I feel my heart pounding, filling with so much anxiety, it feels as if it will burst.

As I grip the edge of my door, letting him see the nerves and apprehension, he asks, "Do you mind if I come in?"

A second passes as I look past him to his cruiser. The pounding inside my chest intensifies.

I don't know what to do, and I'm terrified to make the wrong decision.

"Is this a bad time?" he asks when I don't answer, his voice carrying my attention back to him.

The light blue eyes that pierce into me tell me it's all right, there's a kindness there, a caring soul somewhere deep inside. A small voice inside my head is screaming at me to tell him about Jase. The voice says I'll be safe. There will be no debt, and all of this will be over.

But a bigger side, the side of me that's taken over, the side I don't recognize, isn't ready for this to end. Already I love being touched by Jase Cross. I crave for that powerful man to use me, and I'm determined to use him in return to get answers.

I can practically hear his sinful voice, luring me into a darkness I may never come out of.

And that's why I tell him, "I'm sorry, it's just a bad time. I wasn't expecting anyone."

The officer nods his head in understanding, but his eyes are assessing and my body tenses. *Just go. Please, go.*

"I'm new here," he tells me. "I came down from upstate New York."

I nod, blinking away the confusion. I anticipated him saying goodbye and apologizing, but instead he shuffles his feet on my porch, shoving his hands into his pockets as he speaks.

"I wanted to come to a smaller city, somewhere with fewer problems and a slower pace."

A genuine, soft sound of amusement comes from me, forcing the semblance of a smile to my lips. "You aren't going to find that here," I tell him.

"So I noticed. Born and raised?" he asks, and I nod.

"My mom moved here when she was pregnant with my sister, before I was born. It was just us three for the longest time."

"Your sister who just passed?" he asks, inflecting his tone with an appropriate amount of sympathy as his voice lowers, and again I only nod. With the small movement comes a pang in my chest. Every reminder of her is like hearing the news that she's missing all over again. Or worse, the news that they found her and my worst fear was realized.

"I'm sorry. I lost my brother a while ago. We were close, so I can understand the loss."

I have to look up to the sky, letting out a slow exhale to keep from tearing up. He doesn't know. No one could know what we went through this past year.

"I'm getting the lay of the land here, and it seems like there may be a bit of trouble from a man who owns a vehicle spotted at your address recently."

My teeth sink into my bottom lip and I try to keep my expression neutral until I can ask, "Who would that be?"

"Jase Cross. His entire family and a few others are

associated with murder and drug rings, along with other criminal activity."

Silence.

It's a long moment that passes, a frigid gust of wind traveling between us before I tell him, "Like I said, this isn't a good time for me."

Officer Walsh takes a large step forward, coming close enough to startle me. Staring into my eyes as my lungs are paralyzed, he lowers his voice and says, "I can help you, Bethany. All you have to do is tell me that's what you want."

Thump. Thump.

Staring into his light blue eyes, feeling the authority that comes off him in waves, I can't speak. I only know when I do say something, no matter what I say, there's a very large probability that I'm going to regret the words that come out of my mouth.

CHAPTER
11

Jase

T HE DOOR OPENS BEFORE THE KNUCKLES OF
my loosely curled fist can even hit the hard wood.
The bite of the cold night nips at my neck at the
same time the warmth of Beth's home welcomes me into
34 Holley Drive.

I'm only slightly aware of either, and neither could
beckon me inside the way Bethany's eyes do. Wide and
cautious, but curious more than anything. In this split
second, the way she's breathing, heavy with anticipation—
nothing's ever made me so fucking excited.

"Jase." She murmurs my name, but not in a greeting.
It's more like an omen.

As I take a step inside, dropping the duffle bag just
inside the foyer, she takes a step back, releasing the door
and allowing me to close it. It's quiet; the only sound is the

foreboding click of the door shutting.

Bethany nervously picks under her nails as she waits silently.

"You scared?" I ask her and she responds with a huff of a sarcastic laugh and the faintest hint of a smile that comes and goes.

"Is that your question?" she asks me and it's then that I catch something's off. Something happened. Squaring my shoulders, I peek behind her. The front hall leads to the kitchen in the back, with the living room to the left and the dining room to the right. It's all quiet, all dark with the exception being the living room.

"If it's my turn to ask a question ... who do I remind you of?"

My gaze returns slowly to her. I let it travel down her body, noting that she's in sweats and a baggy t-shirt that reads, *Coffee Solves Everything*.

"No questions yet," I answer her and then brush her thick locks of gently curled hair behind her back. "You need to see what I want from you first."

She leans her weight onto her left heel, tilting her stance and the nervousness wanes some. That's better.

"I think I got a good idea of that last night," she says and tries to hide the breathiness that came with "last night" and the rosy blush that slowly rises to her cheeks.

My smirk kicks up, and a warmth flows through me. I knew she needed it. I knew she'd love to be played with.

Lowering my lips to hers, but just barely keeping our mouths from touching, I look her in the eyes and tell her, "That was hardly a nibble of what's to come."

Instead of stepping back slightly as I expect her to do

so I'm not in her space, she stands her ground and shrugs as she replies, "No need to hold back tonight." Her words caress my face, causing a longing desire to travel down my body, all the way to my cock.

Keeping my gaze pinned on her, I stand up straighter and gesture to the living room. "After you then," I offer.

"Not in the bedroom?" she comments under her breath as she walks ahead of me, and I don't hesitate to grab her hip in my left hand and pull her back into my chest. Her yelp of surprise only makes me harder.

With my lips at her ear, I whisper, "The bedroom is reserved for the nights you beg me the second I walk in to fuck that pretty little cunt of yours."

The second the words are spoken, I let her go and she falls forward slightly. Barely catching herself although she plays it off, just like she tried to hide her lust for me as she walks ahead of me. I watch her wide hips sway and grab the black duffle bag I'd dropped by the door.

"What's that?" she asks when she sees it, taking a seat on the sofa easily. As if she's not nervous at all, and that moment a few seconds ago never happened. It's cute that she thinks she's playing hard to get when she's nothing but eager.

"Rope, for starters." Her eyes flash, but she says nothing more.

The bag drops with a thud and as the sound of the zipper opening fills the room, she leans closer, attempting to peek inside.

"Ethanol?" she questions with a hint of hesitancy as I pull out several feet of thin nylon rope.

"I'm not sure we'll need that tonight," I tell her absently

as I let the rope fall to a puddle on the floor and move the coffee table out of the middle of the room. It drags along the floor, and in true Beth fashion she focuses on the bag, walking to it and taking into account everything inside.

A bottle of ethanol, a lighter, candles, a torch, balm, four sections of nylon rope, two large flame-retardant blankets, a weighted blanket, and last but not least, a knife.

Her lips purse as she stiffens by the bag. The worst thing that could happen is that I scare her off. I've never wanted anything more than I want this right now.

"Don't be scared," I tell her softly with a bit of humor I know will challenge her.

"I'm not," she bites back, even though she is. I can see it.

"If you could supply a bucket of ice, I think you'll be grateful for that."

At my words, she turns her head slowly toward me.

"What exactly is this?" she asks softly, backing away from the bag.

"I'm going to show you."

Her eyes move to the digital clock and she says, "Eight fourteen…"

"We'll start the clock at eight if you'd like," is all I offer her.

When I stand up, the coffee table now repositioned, her arms are crossed and she's staring down at the bag.

"Your reluctance is understandable, but I promise you, you want this." My last word hisses in the air, the tempting snake that led Eve to the apple.

"I want at least one question answered first," she tells me, lifting her gaze from the bag to meet my own.

"One."

"What kind of business is done at The Red Room?" she asks and a glimmer of a smile pulls at my lips.

"Once you're tied up with your hands behind your head, I'll allow you to ask the question again, and I'll answer it completely."

The skepticism is there, the hesitation, but slowly she stands tall and leaves the living room, heading to the kitchen. Presumably she's getting the ice.

I lay down the first flame-retardant blanket and leave the second within reach.

Beth makes her way back into the room holding a glass wine decanter filled with ice. "I don't have an ice bucket," she admits to me while I'm still on my knees, fixing the corner of the blanket.

"You nervous?" I ask her, reaching for the decanter.

"You fucking know I am." She rushes her words like she can't get them out fast enough, and a deep, rough chuckle leaves me.

"I'm going to need you naked for this," I tell her as I set the ice down next to the folded-up blanket.

"Of course you are," she says skeptically, turning away from me and breathing out deep as she shakes out her hands.

"If you want to stop, it stops. I'll learn your limits. You'll still get your answers and your debt paid." I start with addressing her logical concerns, but move to the other side of her thoughts. "The exotic becomes the erotic. Have you ever heard of that?" I ask her.

"I understand temperature play and that this is meant to be ..." she trails off and swallows as she turns to face me, her features riddled with a mix of nervousness and fear. "Why like this?"

"Because I crave this," I admit to her without thinking twice. "It soothes a part of me that isn't easily kept at bay. I will enjoy every second of this. It's worth more to me than secrets and a debt." I didn't realize how much I needed this, how much I coveted her body beneath mine as I brought out the most intense reactions from her until those words were spoken.

Her eyes close and her body trembles.

"Does this excite you?" I ask her and when I do, her hands move under the hem of her baggy shirt, to the top of her sweatpants and she slowly pushes them down, stepping out of them and then opening her eyes.

Her lips part slightly, ready to answer. But she closes herself off, shutting her mouth and balling her hands into fists at her side. Clearing her throat, she looks away and I remind her, "I'll answer your question tonight, the single question. But after tonight, it's tit for tat. Tonight is so you can see what I want."

She nods her head once and then again, standing only feet from me in nothing but her socks and a t-shirt. "Yes, it excites me," she finally answers and as she does, the radiator kicks on behind her, making her jump slightly.

"And it scares you?" I ask, although it's more of a statement. She doesn't waste a second to answer, nodding furiously.

"I don't like not being in control. Tied up and..." She doesn't finish her thought, and swallows thickly.

"You're thinking too much," I tell her and her gaze narrows. All the jitters leave her in that instant and I have to smile. "There you go, just remember how much you hate me and this should be easy."

With her lips pressed in a thin line, she removes her socks first and then reaches behind her back to unhook her bra, revealing a simple white cotton bra with no lace, no frills, no padding.

And with her arms crossed in front of her, she prepares to lift her shirt over her head, but I stand abruptly and stop her, gripping her wrists.

Her skin is hot to the touch.

"I want to do it," I tell her softly. Slowly, she releases her grip on the hem and I circle her, taking my time to observe how the shirt, hitting just below her ass, is more tempting than I'm sure she thought it would be.

"You didn't try to impress me, did you?" I ask, although the light in the room shines off her freshly shaved legs, smooth and glimmering.

"This is business, Cross," she tells me and I simply nod.

"It is."

Making sure not to touch her skin, I grip her hem and lift the shirt above her head, revealing one inch of skin at a time. The movement is achingly slow. Her body quivers as I let a single finger run along her side. The lone touch causes such a strong reaction in her, and it only makes me that much harder for her.

She doesn't look at me; instead she stares straight ahead, but she doesn't cover herself either.

She's fucking beautiful. Every inch of her. From the freckle on her lower stomach, to the pale rose pink of her nipples. Her hips are wide enough to grip during a

punishing fuck, and her ass begs me to smack those perfect curves.

Time ticks as I circle her one more time. "You're beautiful," I whisper and the small compliment does wonders
in relaxing her stiff posture. "How long has it been since
someone's told you that?" I ask her, standing in front of her
and allowing my gaze to roam to her hazel eyes.

She blinks and her lashes seem thicker, her lips fuller,
her chestnut hair ready to be fisted as I kiss her. Everything
about her is fuckable and desirable.

"I don't know," she whispers. Her eyes drift to the blanket and then look back to me. "It's been a long time."

I search her expression for an idea of just how long,
but she doesn't give an answer.

"Lie down on the blanket."

Her shoulder brushes my arm as she obeys.

The blanket moves under her slightly, but her entire
body is positioned in the center of it.

Using the longest section of the thin rope, I lift up her
thighs, making her knees bend so I can lay the middle of
the rope under her ass. I secure her hands with the remainder of the rope on either side of her with a simple bondage
knot. I'm effectively making sure she won't be able to reach
up. Half the rope is knotted around her left wrist where it
slips under her thighs, right below her plush ass and the
other half is knotted around her right wrist. Perfect.

"I'm going to put a weighted blanket across your ankles," I tell her as I pull it out of the bag, reaching past the
sealed bottle of ethanol and one of the two candles.

"Why?" she asks, and I answer easily in an attempt to
calm her nerves. "So you'll have a resistance to lifting them

up. It'll make everything feel more intense."

With the weighted blanket laying across her ankles, she's bared to me, bound and somewhat calmer than I imagined.

"You fought very little tonight," I note.

"Learning the ropes," she answers softly, opening her eyes for the first time since she looked down and saw the rope twined around her wrists.

"You're going to enjoy this," I tell her, lightly brushing my fingers down her stomach. When I do, I hear the weighted blanket rustle, but her legs stay still, immobilized from the weight. Her shoulders shudder and her head lifts slightly before falling back down into a halo of brunette hair.

"I'm ready for you to answer my question," she says confidently. As if we're in an interview and she's not bound on her living room floor, available for me to do whatever I'd like to her.

Her breasts are perky and full; taking them in my hand, I play with their weight and bend down to suck her nipple into my mouth. I moan around her nipple and then let my teeth drag up them. One, and then the other.

Bethany lets her back arch and her body sways to the side, moving further from me as she puts her weight on her left hip. Pushing her back down on the blanket, I blow across her nipple, chilling the moisture I left there and she sucks in a shuddered breath, her head falling back and a sweet sound of rapture leaving her lips.

"I'm going to take my time touching you, playing with you," I say without acknowledging her earlier remark. "Does that scare you?"

"What are you going to use from the bag?" she asks me and a slight laugh slips from my lips.

"That doesn't answer my question."

"My answer relies on it." Her eyes darken, her pupils dilating as she answers me honestly. I can see the plea in her eyes to not push her boundaries, to not touch the bag of supplies.

She should know better than that.

"Everything, Bethany. I intend on taking full advantage of tonight."

Bethany

I'm scared, I can't deny that. My entire body is alive with both fear and something else. Something sinful.

Every tiny hair on my body, from head to toe, is standing on end. My nipples have hardened and every touch from Jase sends a trail of goosebumps down my body that makes me shiver with hunger for more.

More of his warm breath on my chilled skin, more of his fingers barely touching my sides as he brings them down to my hips.

But only if he answers me. He'd better fucking answer me. *We have a deal.*

"What kind of business do you do at The Red Room?" I ask him as he turns his attention away from me and reaches to the decanter of ice.

He makes me wait for my answer, but not too long.

"I first created The Red Room as a place to conduct other business. My brother's business, really."

His voice is far too low, too soothing and seductive for the information he's relaying. The ice clinks in the glass before he places a single piece at my lips.

I part my lips, intent on sucking the ice, but he moves it too soon, tracing my lips and then bringing it lower. A cold sensation flows over my skin in a wave.

"Eager thing, aren't you?" he teases me.

"Fuck you." The words come out quickly but his are just as quick as he says, "Only when you beg me, cailín tine." I don't know why he calls me that, *cailín tine*. Or what it means. And I hate that I swallow down my curiosity rather than ask him. But I want him to answer my damn question.

"My brother was dealing. Drugs, guns, all sorts of things," he tells me and my focus returns to the one reason I have to allow this. The one logical reason I'd ever willingly put myself in this situation. *Jenny*.

I ready myself for another question to clarify, but Jase places a finger over my lips. His touch is so hot compared to the ice. "I'm still answering. Let me tell you everything," he whispers.

He runs another cube from the dip just below my throat, down the center of my chest. His hand brushes my breast until he brings the ice farther, all the way to my belly button, circling it and then moving lower still, letting it sit just where my thighs meet.

The ice itself is numbingly cold, sending a spike of awareness through my body. But it's the path that I'm so highly aware of. Each trail leaves a bit of water behind and the air cools it, causing every nerve ending there to prepare to spark.

Even though he lets the ice linger at the top of my pussy, he's quick to repeat the pattern, and I don't know how it's possible, but it makes my body feel even hotter. My toes curl on the third round, and my core heats.

All I can do is turn my head, close my eyes and my fists, and try not to let the ice excite me.

It's an impossible feat, though.

In between every round, he gives me more information, and occasionally asks me insignificant things. Things I don't mind answering, all the while Jase promises to tell me more. It's not quite tit for tat, since he's giving me more and more information about The Red Room and what happened to make it become what it is, all while asking me simple questions that don't require more than one-word answers. But he's gauging how my body reacts when I tell the truth. Taking the time to learn my body. My only response to that is that I'm not a liar. I don't have the time to tell him that though as he continues to feed me information.

"I enjoyed the control. Knowing when and where everyone would meet up. Giving them a space where they could enjoy themselves, and observing them in the meantime. I wanted to know the ins and outs of every partner we had. I wanted their secrets…"

I can barely breathe as he gives me his past so easily, all while bringing the mostly melted ice down farther than he ever has to my pussy, and gently pushing it inside of me. My lips make a perfect O as every nerve ending in my body lights.

He continues his story as my lips part, feeling the rush of desire spark inside of my body. "So we could blackmail them. I used the bar to set everyone up to owe us in some way, or to have information we could use against both our partners and our enemies. In this industry, everyone is an enemy at some point, and we would be ready the second anyone thought they could turn their backs on us."

It's exhilarating.

Both his touch, and the tale of how they rose to power. Creating a place for divine pleasures and allowing everyone to taste, for everyone to fall into their grasp to be controlled and their actions predicted so easily.

He lowers his lips to the crook of my neck, letting his warm breath be at odds with the chill that's slowly melting at my core, being consumed with his criminal touch.

"I sell every addiction possible and I don't have rules within those walls." As he speaks, he pushes his fingers inside of me, dragging them against my front wall and bringing me closer and closer to the peak of an impending orgasm. I close my eyes tight, trying not to give in although I know it's useless. My toes have curled and the pleasure builds inside of me so quickly like a raging storm, unstoppable and demanding its damage be done.

"Every corner of that place is defiled; every square inch has been touched by sin. That's the kind of business I conduct in The Red Room."

My neck arches as I give in to the need, a wave of pleasure rising from my belly outward, followed by another, a harsher, more severe wave crashing through me. I can't move an inch as Jase grips my throat with his free hand and continues to torture me, fucking me with his fingers and drawing out every bit of my orgasm. I wish I could move. I want to get away from the third wave threatening to consume me, but I'm paralyzed as it rages through me.

Every nerve ending in my body ignites, my body shuddering and trembling as my release takes its time, wandering through my body and slowly dissipating. Jase removes his fingers carefully, and I gasp in pleasure as he circles my clit before bringing his fingers to his mouth.

My arousal shines on his fingers as he sucks it off, one by one. I can't bring myself to look away when he groans in sheer delight.

Even as my heart races and adrenaline and excitement race through me, fear freezes my body when Jase picks up a knife from his bag. It's only a pocket knife.

It's just to get the ropes off, I tell myself. It's amazing how the sight of it destroys the previous moment. I close my eyes, waiting to hear the sound of the blade sawing at the rope, but Jase doesn't allow me to.

"I need your eyes open for this. You need to stay still and I don't want the touch to startle you." He sounds so calm and in control as he splays a hand on my chest. His elbow rests on my shoulder and pins me in place as my heart lurches inside of me, ready to escape.

My gaze begs him to explain, to stop, to reconsider whatever he's doing as he brings the knife closer to me.

"It's only to shave the small hairs from your body," he says, answering my unspoken questions. "I won't hurt you," he tells me soothingly as the blade just barely touches my skin. He drags it slowly across my breast, all the way down my mound and then back up, avoiding my sensitive, swollen nub.

"Can I let you go?" he asks me, gently lifting his elbow. "Or are you going to move?"

I can only swallow, I can barely even comprehend what he's saying since the panic is so alive within me.

"If you move, it will cut you," he tells me.

"I'll be still," I whisper and as the blade lowers to my skin I consider the word, stop. So easy to say. I could say it; it's right there, waiting to be spoken. But Jase drags the knife along my chest before I can utter it and then he kisses the sensitized skin. An open-mouth kiss that feels like everything. Like this is the way a kiss is meant to be, and every other way is wrong.

My head's fuzzy and a haze clouds it as he scrapes the knife along my body, leaving a pink path occasionally, but his kisses and the ice make the evidence vanish.

It's all overwhelming and agonizingly slow. By the time he gets to my pussy, I'm on the edge of another release. My impending orgasm is waiting for the knife, for his touch, for a kiss. But it doesn't come.

After the longest time, my body feels his absence and I open my eyes. He pours ethanol onto a rag, then wipes down my body in one swift stroke and before I can say anything, a flame lights on a candle and he lowers it to the ethanol, lighting my skin ablaze.

The scream is trapped in the split second, but before its escape, his hand follows the path, quenching the heat and leaving me wide eyed and breathless.

So hot, and then so cold.

With a pounding heart, I take in the reality. "You lit me on fire."

"No, I lit the alcohol just above your skin on fire." He does it again and this time hot wax drips with it and I suck in a tight breath, my hands turning to fists from the slight

119

pain, the immediate heat, and the cold absence that comes afterward. My head thrashes from side to side as he does it again and again. The pain morphing to unmatched pleasure makes my body feel alive in a way I never knew was possible.

Every climax feels higher and more unbearable than the last. My words fail me as Jase moves down my body, not sparing any inch of my skin.

The alcohol, the fire, his touch. Over and over. He massages the wax onto my breasts before using the knife to pick it off, and the third time he does it, I cum violently.

The pleasure rages through my body with no evidence of it even approaching until the blinding pleasure rocks through me, from my belly to the tip of my toes and fingers.

It's as if my body has rebelled, choosing his touch and this heat over any sense of calm. It prefers the chaos, the unknown, the absence of all control and stability.

With my bottom lip still quivering and my belly trembling as the tremors of the aftershock subside, Jase kisses me, madly and deeply. I feel all of him in this kiss and it kills me that I can't lift my hands up, keeping him where I want him.

I'm at his mercy. Fully and truly, and that very fact plays tricks on me. Telling me I love it. Telling me he knows what I need more than I do.

With every pleasure still ringing in me, he pulls away and stands up, removing his shirt and the light from the candle plays along the lines of his defined muscles. I can see his thick length pressing against his zipper and when he palms it, I have to look away. I'm so close to another orgasm. My clit is throbbing; I feel swollen and used, but he's hardly touched me there.

The sound of a zipper makes me look back at him and the instant I do, his pants, along with his belt, drop to the floor with a clink and a thud and his dick is all I can see.

His girth is so wide I'm not sure I could wrap my hand around him. I can practically feel the veins pressing against my walls and pulling every ounce of pleasure from me, practically imagine his rounded head sliding back and forth over my clit. Oh my God. He's massive. He grabs his cock and rubs the glistening precum over the head and that's when I lose it.

Cumming again, and he didn't even touch me. That's how much power he has over me. Just the thought of what he could do to me, how he could ruin me, how he is so much more than any boy I ever thought of letting touch me... all of it is fuel that ignites a raging fire inside.

Jase groans deep in the back of his throat, dropping to the floor so quickly and so hard, I know it will leave bruises on his knees. "Cum again," he commands me breathlessly, leaning over my body to kiss and bite the crook of my neck as he pushes three fingers inside of me and ruthlessly fucks me with them.

The waves of my last release have barely left me when the next orgasm crashes through me, harder and higher than any of those before. My scream is silent, my body stiff as it commands attention from all of me. My body, my soul.

And Jase doesn't stop, even as my arousal leaks down my ass, he continues. Even as I feel myself tighten around his fingers, he doesn't stop.

I can't. I can't take it. I can't breathe.

I can't move. I can't speak.

I'm helpless and consumed by fire and lust.

I try to focus on Jase when he whispers in my ear, but my body won't stop shaking and my neck is rigid. "When you look at me, know this is what I want from you. Only I can give you this." His words hiss in the air, crackling and demanding to be burned in my memory.

Jase Cross destroyed me and what I thought was pleasure.

And where I thought my boundaries lied with him.

CHAPTER
12

Bethany

M Y EYES OPEN QUICKLY, THE DARKNESS
consuming me except for the moonlight from
the bedroom windows. My heart's racing and
it's then that I realize the trembling isn't a dream. I can't
stop shaking and I'm so fucking cold.

"Shhh." Jase's voice is anything but calming. After the
initial shock of realizing he's in bed with me, I barely turn
around before the bed groans and he pulls the weighted
blanket up and around my entire body.

Frantically I try to recount it all, every moment that I
can remember.

"What did you do to me?" I ask, and the question
comes out viciously. I'm fucking freezing, and I can't stop
trembling.

"I brought you to bed," he says lowly, a threat barely

there, warning me to be careful but fuck that.

"What did you do?" The words are torn from my throat. It's not even the fear that's the most overwhelming. As my throat dries and a sinking sensation in my stomach takes over, I look him in the eyes and realize how much trust I had in him. It wasn't just business. I gave up more than I should have, and he did something to me. He hurt me.

How could you? I want to say the words, but I can't bear to bring them up and admit to the both of us that I thought he wouldn't hurt me. That I was that fucking naïve.

Jase's arm is heavy and pulls me closer to him, even though I attempt to push him away as he says, "It's just the endorphins crashing." Although his words are drenched with irritation, there's something else there, something buried deep down low in his words that I can't decipher. "You're okay," he nearly whispers and then pulls me in closer, dragging my ass to his groin, my back to his chest and nuzzling the nape of my neck with the tip of his nose. "It's okay, I've got you."

His voice is a calming balm. Even as I continue to shake. As my fingers feel numb and then like they're on fire. Cold again. "I'm so cold."

I almost expect my confession to turn to fog in front of me. Like warm breath in the winter air.

"You were on a high," Jase tells me and then presses his arm against mine, pushing it closer to me and acting as if I'm not trembling uncontrollably. "It's all coming down. I thought you may have a little aftershock. That's why I stayed," he explains.

Aftershock. Endorphins.

He didn't drug me. It's not drugs. I can barely swallow for a long moment, trying to make it stop, but my body's not listening.

"Does this happen all the time?" I ask him, attempting to let go of the anger, swallowing my regret that I immediately assumed the worst of him. It was my first instinct, and shame hits me hard as I realize he did quite the opposite.

I'm a bitch. I am an asshole. An embarrassed asshole.

With sleep lacing his words he tells me, "Not often, but I imagine that was your first?" and I instantly clench my legs. Remembering the ice, the cold, his touch, the fire.

My shoulders beg to buck forward, my eyes closing at the memory and the heat flourishing in my belly.

"Was it?" he teases me, nipping my neck and just that small touch threatens to push me over again.

"I can't," I say, and the words leave me in a single breath. A single plea. Instantly a chill creeps up my neck, the open air finding its place there as Jase moves his head to the other pillow.

A shaky breath leaves me as I turn my head to peek at him, craning my neck as my back is still positioned firmly against his chest. "Did we have sex?" I ask him, feeling a weight press down on my chest.

Jase merely gazes back at me. The depths of his dark eyes deepen as I stare into them. Licking my lower lip first, I explain, "I don't remember everything."

"We didn't. No," he answers me, and his expression remains guarded. "I told you, you'd have to beg me for it."

His warmth calms me and slowly I stop trembling as hard. Very slowly, but the tremors are still there.

"For all I know, I did tell you to fuck me," I tell him.

"You could barely look at me, let alone speak."

"Holy shit," I murmur beneath my breath.

"When I fuck you, trust me when I say you'll remember it."

His words force a shiver of pleasure through me when I remember I saw … I saw *all* of him. "Why am I shaking so much?"

"From you getting off so many times. Your body can only handle so much."

"I can't believe it can feel like that," I say, thinking out loud.

"Sometimes the things that cause you pain can bring you so much pleasure."

"Not everything that brings you pain." The hollowness in my chest expands at my thought, drifting to darker places.

The shaking and trembling stop altogether, but Jase doesn't let me go and I'm happy for that. There's so much comfort in being held right now.

"Tell me something," I ask Jase, resting my cheek into the pillow, feeling the warmth come back to me and the lull of sleep ready to pull me under once again.

"Tell you something?" He ponders and then readjusts on the bed, making it shake slightly. "What do you want to know?"

"Anything," I answer as my eyelids fall heavily without second-guessing and my eyes pop open wider, remembering all the bits and pieces he told me about The Red Room. "Maybe about your brothers?"

Once again Jase's lips find my neck, and this time he leaves an open-mouthed kiss there. I'm starting to love those kinds of kisses. I think they're my favorite. "I had four brothers, now I have three and I recently learned that my younger brother, the one I was closest with…" He hesitates and again that small space on my neck feels the prickle of the air instead of his warmth. "I found out his death wasn't an accident; it was murder. And it was supposed to be me, not him."

"Oh my God," I whisper, completely shocked. My heart breaks in half for him. I know the pain of losing a sibling, the agony of blaming yourself. But knowing it was supposed to be you instead? "I'm so sorry." I put every ounce of sincerity into my words and pray it doesn't come out the way everyone else says, like the people who say it simply because they don't know what else to say. "I'm really sorry."

Jase doesn't say anything at all. Not for a while until he requests the same from me. "Tell me something."

"I can't figure you out, Jase," I answer him almost immediately.

"You already know who I am, cailín tine. Don't let me fool you."

I look over my shoulder to ask him, "What's that mean? Cailín tine?"

He gives me one of those smirks, but it's almost sad and short lived. "Fiery girl."

My entire body betrayed me earlier, and so does my heart in this moment, beating just for him with a warmth I've never felt before.

As I nuzzle back down into the pillow, I remember Officer Walsh and I spit out the words before I hide them forever. "A cop came asking about you today. He knocked at my door."

Nerves prick down my neck, but Jase's touch remains soothing and his voice calm when he asks, "What was his name?"

"Cody Walsh," I answer and then feel Jase's nod as his nose runs along my neck.

"He won't be a problem. He's just new."

"Don't you want to know what I told him?"

"If you want to tell me."

"I didn't tell him anything."

His response is to kiss my neck. Then my jaw. He tries to lie back down, leaving my lips wanting but I take them with my own. Reaching up to grip the back of his neck, and pulling myself off the comfort of the bed.

It's a quick kiss, but it was mine to have. And mine to give.

"What was that for?" he asks me, and I answer him honestly. "I wanted you to have it."

Turning my back to him, I lie back under the covers. There are no more questions or conversations. With my eyes wide open, I pretend to sleep. After a short while, the bed protests under the weight of him moving, the covers are shrugged off behind me and I listen to him leave. Across the wooden floorboards, down the stairs. I can only faintly hear him in the living room, but I recognize the sound of the front door opening and closing.

All the while, there's this vise wrapped around my heart. Keeping it still, not allowing it to move the way it used to.

CHAPTER
13

Jase

"WHAT HAPPENED TO HER? TO Jennifer Parks?"

Seth hesitates. Seated across from me, he slides forward to readjust before leaning back into an auburn leather armchair. It's silent in the back of The Red Room. Not a single beat of the music or murmur of the guests makes its way through these doors.

Nothing makes it out of them either.

It's a decadent but vacant space. A simple, but too-fucking-expensive iron and driftwood desk with no drawers stands in the middle of the room. My chair is at one end, while two matching chairs are on the other side. Not a damn thing else in the room.

The stubble on my jaw is rough; I'm way past due for a shave as I run my hand along my jaw as I wait for

Seth's answer.

"I'm still working on it, but let me tell you what I've got so far."

"Are you fucking kidding me?" The rage is inexplicable as I slam the edge of my fist down on the desk. It jolts and I clench my jaw, hating that something like this can get to me.

I focus on calming my shit down, ignoring the irritation and Seth's questioning gaze.

All day I've been on edge. Ever since I left Bethany's place, the second the sun rose.

"It goes deeper than you think, Boss." His voice is low, testing my patience and apologetic even.

"Let me have it," I speak and gesture for him to get going.

"She went missing on December twenty-eighth, but before then she was in and out of her sister's home and several friends' places. It was January seventeenth that the burned remains, including several of her teeth, were found in a trunk at the bottom of the Rattle River on the west side of town."

I remember the flash of an image I found myself, searching through the archives at the downtown station hard drive. It was all the information Kent, one of the detectives we keep on our payroll, had to give.

"Fucking brutal," I murmur. The remains were charred, but some of the bones were broken before being burned.

"She was tortured, but time of death couldn't be determined."

"I already know this. Get to something I don't know."

He starts to speak, but before he can even suck in the

air needed for the first word, I ask, "Did you find anything on the sister?"

My fingers rap on the desk, one at a time with brief pauses, one after the other. As if it's only a casual conversation.

"Bethany Fawn?"

At my nod, he begins. "Jennifer was born out of wedlock to a Catherine Parks. Shortly after her birth, her mother and father got hitched, then conceived Bethany. Not long after her birth, the father took off. Leaving their mom with no job, a toddler and an infant."

"Where did he go?"

"Nebraska, where he died of a heart attack in a casino three years ago."

"Did they keep in touch?"

"Not a word," Seth answers professionally, but his eyes are questioning.

"Go on."

"Bethany Fawn, the younger of the two, did well in school. And it seems like that was all she was interested in. She's a nurse on the psych ward at Rockford. She's worked there since she graduated. Apparently her mother had issues in the last years of her life and she chose this path because of it. Her sister--"

"What issues?" Again, I cut him off midbreath.

"Alzheimer's."

"How old was she?"

"Bethany? Twenty. Her mother was fifty-two when she died."

I watched my mother die slowly, but I was young. Cancer is a bitch. I can only imagine being more aware and having to go through that. Being old enough to under-stand. Back when I was a kid, I was sure Mom was going to get better. Knowing there is no getting better and having to watch someone you love slowly die? That's a cruel way to live. A cruel way to die as well. But that's life, isn't it?

"One thing you may find interesting is that she was spotted with you recently," Seth says and sits back further in his seat. It's the only note on her in the entire depart-ment. "*A possible associate.*"

"And who put that in? Our new friend, Walsh?" I surmise.

"You got it," he says and snaps his fingers. "And you two aren't the only ones doing some digging. Miss Fawn's search history is interesting ... limited, but interesting."

"Is that right?" I ask, bringing my thumb up to run along my chin.

"Little Miss Fawn was looking you up and Officer Walsh after he paid her a visit."

I shrug impatiently, and Seth continues.

"She didn't find much, obviously, since there's nothing on the internet to find... although it seems she's interested in Angie. She's searching for pictures of her, doesn't look like she knows her name. *Jase Cross with brunette. Jase Cross lover. Jase Cross date.* Things like that."

"Angie?" The only piece of information that surprises me so far is this. "Why?"

"I guess she saw her with you in pictures online. But she doesn't have her name, or any information on her."

Who do I remind you of? I remember her question last night. That's why.

"Shit." I breathe out the word. "Anything else?" I ask

him, ignoring the dread, the regret, the deep-seated hate for myself because of everything that happened four years ago. All of those ghosts belong in the past. They can stay there too.

Seth passes me a folder; opening it up reveals six profiles. All are of women in their late twenties, and two I recognize from the club. Jennifer is the first. The second is Miranda. She's gotten thrown out a handful of times. Too high to know she was messing with the wrong guys. Causing problems that aren't easy to fix.

"She ran with quite a crowd," I comment as I sift through the papers, reading one charge after the next and notes about the men they each were associated with. Men I don't trust or like.

"You could say that. It was all recent though. She only came into the scene this past year," Seth comments and leans back in his seat. The leather protests as he does. "College grad who struggled to keep a job after school. Taking one after the next. All had nothing to do with her degree."

"Quit or fired?"

"She quit them all. Everyone I talked to said they loved her, but they knew she wasn't going to stay long. It wasn't *interesting* enough for her," he says but forms air quotes around the word "interesting."

"You think that's why she quit them? Boredom?"

"I'm guessing she just needed to pay her bills." He shrugs. "From what I gather she was eccentric and wanted to solve the world's problems. The last job she had was working at The Bistro across the turnpike."

That particular information catches my attention and

I look up from the papers to see Seth nodding. "Romano's place?"

"The one and only."

Just hearing that name makes me grit my teeth. "He's a dead man." My throat tightens as I speak. All I can see when I hear the word Romano is the picture of Tyler, dead on the wet asphalt; the water soaked into my hoodie he wore that day.

It was supposed to be me.

"Damn right," Seth says and I check my composure. Refusing to let that fuck get in the way of this conversation.

"So, The Bistro," I say to push Seth to continue the conversation, picking at the pages in the folder, and trying to rid my mind of the sight of Tyler. He was a good kid. That's the worst part. No one really deserves to die, but if anyone in this world could have been spared, it should have been him.

Tossing the folders down onto the desk, I lean back, letting the information sink in. "So she's got debt from college, can't get the right job yet so she's bouncing around to pay the bills. She lands a job at The Bistro and something there's leading these girls down a dark path.

"We have eyes down there; what'd they say?" My voice rises on its own, demanding information.

Seth winces slightly before telling me, "You aren't going to like this."

"Don't be a little bitch," I tell him, losing my patience.

"They said she was there and gone. She was friendly and nice, but then up and quit. Miranda was working there at the same time and quit with her. No reason. She didn't stand out and nothing did about the two of them leaving.

Just two open waitress spots to fill when they left."

"So they've got nothing?" I ask as my heart rate rapidly increases and the blood rushes in my ears. "We have a group of women," I enunciate each word and Seth takes the opportunity to butt in.

"Two of them working there at the same time and quitting at the same time," he adds and I meet his gaze, daring him to interrupt me again.

"A group of women with no prior history of any of this bullshit, getting hooked on some shit, all of them racking up charges in the past year and some of them stepping foot into my club. And you're telling me the boys we're paying to watch that shithole have no fucking idea what happened, or who influenced this shit?" I slam the bottom of my oxfords again on the inside of my walnut desk, kicking it as hard as I can on impulse. Needing to get out the rage. My muscles are tense, my body's hot and I need to beat the shit out of something.

I have no fucking impulse control, no restraint today. Not a damn thing keeping me under control.

Moving my chair back into place, I set my elbows on my desk, lower my head and smooth my hand over the back of my neck.

"I'm losing my patience," I tell him. Staring at my desk, I admit the obvious. "I don't like not having answers when I want them. She's one girl. A girl we've seen; a girl we've watched before. We should know who the fuck killed her and why."

Seth grips the armrest, looking away from me, toward the blood-red leather walls that line the room.

"It's like someone's hiding it," Seth speaks quickly.

"Hiding?"

"I can't find a damn thing on her after she started working there other than what we had already with the sweets," he says, and his frustration grows with each word.

"We know she was buying our shit in bulk, high on what was obviously coke. She gave the name of a fake brother when we questioned her, that was early December. Then there's not a trace of her."

"She ever come back after that night?" I ask him. I remember that night. Carter came down here, looking for answers about his drug. It hardly sold shit, it's something that puts you to sleep. We only push it on addicts that can't handle any more. It knocks their asses out as they go through withdrawal. They always come back though, but never for the sweets.

Not until recently.

"No. She never came back and the demand for the sweets dropped simultaneously."

"She was buying for someone," I remark. "Someone who backed off when they found out we were onto them…. maybe that's who did this? He wanted her silenced so there were no loose threads?"

"It's not Romano, we have ears on him, we would know. I've been through every fucking recording from December twenty-seventh to the fucking week she was discovered. He didn't say a word about it. I don't think she's on his radar."

"So it's just a fucking coincidence that all her shit starts going downhill when she starts working for him?" I raise my finger, feeling the lines in my forehead deepen with anger.

"He got her hooked; I think he did. Or someone there did. I think that's when it started, but her dying... whoever it was, they got to her at his place, and Romano doesn't know about it or even realize someone's taking those girls from him."

The pieces of the puzzle fall slowly into place, giving me the rough edges of a watered-down image someone doesn't want me to see.

"It would be easy if it was Romano; he's already a dead man."

"As soon as this new cop is off our fucking backs, he's dead," I tell him, opening up the folder again to see Jennifer's profile on top and Beth's name listed as her only living relative staring back at me in black and white. "If Officer Cody Walsh doesn't watch his step," I say and lift my gaze from Beth's name, where the tips of my fingers still linger to tell Seth, "he's a dead man too."

CHAPTER
14

Bethany

The Coverless Book
Third Chapter

I'm pretending not to be tired. Like the weight and pull of sleep isn't a constant battle tonight. Every day after seeing the doctor, it's like this. Well, every day for the past five years except today. Today will be the exception, because of Jake. He makes me smile, and just smiling reminds me I still have so much left in me.

"I'm really happy you do this for me," I tell Jake, pulling the blanket around my shoulders a little tighter. We're having a picnic in the backyard overlooking the hill. The spring air brings a strong scent of lilac and I breathe it in. As much as I can, and for as long as I can.

This is what living feels like.

"The soups were perfect," he comments and adds, "I didn't know it'd get this cold at night."

"The summer nights are warmer," I tell him easily and then feel embarrassed. Of course they are, I think inwardly and my stomach stirs with nerves.

"We'll have to do it again in summer then."

The nerves turn to something else and they spread higher up to my chest at Jake's words.

"I'd really like that." I almost whisper the words and then have to clear my throat. As he picks two blades of grass, no doubt to whistle with them again like he showed me earlier, I take a chance.

"Maybe even before summer?" I ask him and lean close to nudge his shoulder with mine. Just a nudge, then I sit back upright, but he's quick to nudge mine against his.

"Definitely before summer too."

Time passes and the sun sets too quickly. I know time is almost up, and that's so bittersweet.

"Are you really sick? Like... like, sick sick?" Jake's question pulls the smile from my face in a single swoop. And the nerves settle back in my stomach. I pick two blades of grass, thinking maybe I could whistle too. But instead I let them fall, and the wind takes them.

"The doctor said I was sick years ago..." Instead of letting any bit show of what I felt that day Mama cried and cried in the car, I actually let out a small laugh. It's only a huff of laughter. Even though I'd like to pretend I'm not affected by the pain of the memory, my eyes gloss over.

"Why are you laughing?" Jake sounds truly concerned, and I'm quick to put a reassuring hand over his. That small move changes everything. The electric spark, the sudden *heat. I'm quick to take my hand back.*

"Sorry, it's just a little joke I tell myself," I explain, shaking off both the memories and the touch with a quick sip of water.

"What do you tell yourself?" he asks skeptically as I set the cup down. I can't take my hand off of it as I nervously peek at him and answer, "That I'm invincible."

His smirk is slow to form, but it grows quickly, turning into a grin. "I like that."

His smile is contagious, and I find myself telling him, "I like that you like it."

I'm still biting down on my bottom lip and hoping I'm not blushing too hard when he looks me in the eyes and responds, "I like you, Emmy. I think I more than like you."

Three days came and went. I got lost in the pages of The Coverless Book, falling in love with both Emmy and Jake, rooting for them as he fell in love with her and she with him. I spent all of yesterday checking in with my patients at work before Aiden told me that wasn't what my leave was for. I spent every waking hour trying to occupy my thoughts and time. All so I wouldn't think about Jase Cross or my sister, and every moment in the months that I lost her.

Every moment I wish I could have changed.

Between the two, I thought about Jase the most. Because it felt better to think of him than her. Choosing pleasure over pain.

Three days went by, and I thought of him every

morning and every night. I started to think I'd made it all up because I didn't hear from him, not one word. Not until this afternoon when I got a text from a number I didn't know, giving me an address signed with "J." Followed shortly by the number of hours we'd already spent together. Eleven. I imagine he must've included the time he was in bed with me. One hundred dollars every ten minutes, six hundred dollars an hour, so I've barely made a dent in the time I owe him.

And I haven't gotten anywhere. I have no new information that sheds light onto what happened to Jenny. He says he didn't do it; I already knew The Red Room was a place for drug deals and a criminal hangout.

Nothing new. Time is stagnant and I can't hold on much longer. I can't rely on someone who isn't coming through.

I made it down the long winding path around the massive estate and parked in the back where Jase told me to; I made it all that way without breathing.

Maybe that's why I feel faint as I shut my car door, the thud echoing in the depths of the thick forest I stared into only days ago. The dark greens are covered by a slight dusting of white as the snow falls gently, creeping into the crevices of everything.

Pulling my scarf a bit tighter, I take the steps one by one to the front door.

Answers. I will get answers. Even if it's only one question at a time. *He has to know something.*

The bite from the wind creeps up quickly as I raise my fist to knock on the door, only to hear a beep and a click before I even touch it. Someone else grants me entry. *He already knows I'm here.*

Warily, I push the large, carved wooden door open, and it glides easily with the softest of pushes.

Thump. My heart slams as I remember the last time I gazed at this wood, but the engravings were upside down as I dangled from Jase's shoulder.

It's only been days, but it feels like everything's changed.

The massive foyer greets me with warmth, but not much else. The lighting of the wrought iron chandelier reflects on the shiny marble floor, radiating wealth with the spiral staircase, but that's all this room contains. It's empty and even in the warmth, even coming in from the blustery weather, it's cold in here.

Click.

The door shuts behind me, and the small sound startles me. My quick gasp echoes in the room.

Clenching my fists, I inwardly scold myself. *Pull it together.*

He's only a man. A man with answers. A man who will bring me justice. Justice Jenny deserves.

A man who is not here. I have no idea where he is. But I'm alone in the foyer.

My lips purse as I breathe out, letting my heavy bag drop to the floor. It's topped with the weighted blanket Jase left.

My gaze moves from window to window, to the heavy front door.

I can't help but to test Jase's statement. That the doors are locked on the inside and there's no way out. Something about Jase makes me feel like he wouldn't lie. Like he doesn't make threats, only promises of what's to come.

I think it's the severity of his presence. The confidence in his banter. Everything is always just so with him. It's how he wants it to be, and everything is exactly that. How he wants.

It's the impression he gives me and that impression is why I pull off my gloves and shove them in my coat pocket. Gripping the knob with both hands, I turn and pull. I yank it harder when it doesn't give, feeling the stretch in my arms from tugging on an unmoving door.

Huffing the stray hair out of my face, I glance up at a small black square, smaller than the size of a sheet of notebook paper. It's digital. Whatever lock he uses, it's digital.

"Fingerprints and hand scans," Jase's voice bellows from the empty hall behind me, forcing me to whip around to face him, my hand on my chest. "That sort of thing," he adds, slipping his hands into his pockets.

"Jesus fuck," I gasp with contempt. "Are you trying to give me a heart attack?"

My heart thumps a *yes*, my core clenches with affirmation and my gaze drifts down his body, agreeing with the two of them.

He's not wearing a suit today. And he looks damn good in his perfectly fitted suits. In jeans and a t-shirt stretched tight across his shoulders, showing off those corded muscles in his arms... he's doing that shit on purpose.

Swallowing down my heart, I try to relax again. "Just testing what you said..." My explanation dies in the air as he stalks closer to me with powerful strides and in a dominating way that almost has me stepping back, bumping my ass into the door. Almost, but I hold my ground.

"Well then, I'm relieved you weren't leaving already," he comments, the words spoken lowly as he stops right in front of me.

The air between us crackles like a roaring fire.

How does he do this to me?

"I like it better when you're an asshole," I speak without thinking. I'm rewarded with a charming smile, and a deep rough chuckle.

"I'll remember that, cailín tine." Holding out his hand, he commands me, "Come."

As I reach for my purse, Jase leans down, grabbing the handle before I can. His blanket is in plain sight on top and before I can speak, he comments, "You could have kept it with you; it may help you sleep."

One step in front of the other I follow him, with only the sounds of our footsteps keeping us company while I try not to think too much about what he said and why.

He doesn't care about my sleep.

He doesn't care about how I'm feeling.

He wants to get his dick wet. He wants to tie me up and do with me what he wishes.

All of this is simply to keep me amenable.

Jase Cross may have the upper hand, but I'm doing this for me.

The echoes of my footsteps get louder in the narrow corridor as I think, *I'm doing this for Jenny.*

One step, one beat of my heart, one tick of the clock.

I have my questions lined up in a pretty row. Without warning, Jase halts and unlocks a door, but how? I don't know. It simply clicks the moment he stops in front of it and with a flick of the handle, it opens.

144

I've never seen wealth like this before. And I imagine it shows in my expression, judging by the smug look on Jase's face when he opens the door wider and says, "After you."

"Where would you like me?" I ask him the moment he opens the door and I step in before taking a look. "Oh," I murmur, and the word leaves my lips without my conscious consent.

The click of the door closing behind me is followed by a dull thud of a lock, some sort of lock, moving into place.

My belly flips in a way I don't understand. Almost like when you're driving down a hill too fast, or on a roller coaster. The anticipation of the fall, the sudden drop of reality making your stomach somersault.

As I spot the table in the middle of the room, that's exactly what I feel. Followed by the same exact cold prickling I remember so well from three nights ago traveling along my skin.

"What do you think?" Jase asks me, and at the same time he reaches up to my shoulders to take my coat. I anticipate the feel of his fingers trailing along my skin as he does, but he's careful not to touch me. I think he does it on purpose.

I think he does more things with intent than I first realized.

"It's not at all like your foyer," I comment and then drag my eyes back to the wooden bench in the middle of the room. It's at odds with the large plush carpet that takes up most of the space. I have to look out further to the edge to note that under it is a barn wood floor, or something like it. A darker wood, with wide planks. The cream rug is the brightest thing in here, and thank goodness it's large.

Even with the three chandeliers at varying heights with a mix of iron and wood, the room has a soft, airy feeling. Dim and romantic even.

As my coat falls off my shoulders, I take a half step forward and touch the wall. It's a thick wallpaper in a damask cream, but it's darkened by the blood-red pattern within it.

Besides the bench and a matching dresser, there's a whiskey-colored leather chaise lounge and a white crystal fireplace that would certainly be the focus, if not for the wooden bench dead smack in the center of it all.

With the flick of a switch from behind me, I hear the gas turn on and the fireplace roars to life. Jase's hand is still on the switch when I peek behind my shoulder.

I dare to step forward and touch the edge of the wooden bench, noting it's lined with padding upholstered in a soft black leather.

"It's beautiful. It's primitive and raw. Elegant, yet seductive in a way that borders on decadence."

He doesn't respond to my comment, although his eyes never leave me as I walk around the table. "The wood won't catch on fire?" I ask him, remembering how the flames felt like they consumed everything. I've never felt so alive.

"It's for fucking, not fire play." Jase's words come with authority and a heat that could match that raging from the fireplace behind me.

My lungs still as I'm pinned by his gaze. "Is that what you think you'll be doing today?"

Thump, thump, thump. The pace picks up.

"I think you'd enjoy it and my temperament hasn't been... appropriate. I'd appreciate a good fuck."

"I can say no," I remind him, feeling the warring need

to give in, to have it all, and to keep my head on straight.

"You could." His dismissive nature would piss me off if it weren't for the way he looks at me. Like he can see right through me, but he doesn't want to. He wants to see *me*.

"I don't fuck every man I find attractive. Even if I'm willing to admit," I pause a moment, wondering if I should say it out loud. It brings the truth to life when you speak it, but he already knows. This cocky bastard is well aware of what's between us. "Even if I'm willing to admit there's chemistry between us and I like what you do to me. If it weren't for the fact that I have questions and a debt you're holding over my head... I wouldn't give you the time of day."

The heat sizzles between us, although the nerves rack through my body. He intimidates me. Maybe it's something I hadn't admitted to myself before, but in this moment, as he stares down at me, making me wait for a response, I'm so sincerely aware of how much he intimidates me.

"Business then?" Jase asks with an arched brow; his expression doesn't hold a hint of emotion, or amusement. He's a man in control and nothing more.

Standing toe to toe with him, I swallow as I nod. "It's business."

"I have the first question, you have the next." He speaks as he turns his back to me and strides to the dresser, laying my coat over the top of it. He stands there a second too long. The silence is only broken by the pop of the fire to the left of him. The bright light sends shadows down the side of him, and when he turns around those shadows make his jawline seem sharper, his eyes darker and every inch of his exposed skin looks taut and powerful.

He exudes raw masculinity.

"Strip." He gives the command and whatever hint of defiance had come over me flees in an instant.

I have to lean down to unzip my leather boots, then slip them off. I'm ashamed to say I put more effort into this outfit than a woman with self-respect would. The dark denim skinny jeans take a little more effort to shimmy out of, and all the while Jase stands there with his muscular arms crossed in front of him as he leans against the dresser, watching in silence.

I can't even look at him as I second-guess everything in this moment.

I'm not a whore, but that's exactly what I feel like. I can't pretend it's anything else.

When I'm left in nothing but my silk undershirt and lace bra, both covered by an oversized, cream cashmere sweater, Jase's steps destroy the distance between us. It only takes three steps until he's in front of me, his hands at the hem of my sweater. I'm quicker than he is, my hands wrapping around his powerful wrists. My arms are locked and my nails nearly dig into his flesh as I glare into his prying gaze.

"I can do it myself," I say, pushing the words through clenched teeth.

"I'm paying very well for this time with you. I intend to enjoy every minute. If you'd like for it to stop, you know how to tell me just that."

There's no reason I should feel a sudden stab of emotions up my throat, drying it and tightening it. Or the hollowness that grows in my chest.

"It's just business, isn't it?" he questions and with

another thump of my treacherous heart, I release his wrists, waiting for him to undress me like he wishes.

Whore. Whore is the first word that comes to mind, and how I made it this long without feeling like one is beyond me.

"May I ask a question then? I know you have yours first, but I'd like to ask one, if you'll … allow it." I keep my tone professional as I can, holding back the desire to smack my hand across his arrogant, handsome face.

Jase doesn't touch my sweater. Instead he walks around me to stand behind me, leaving only the fire for me to look at. His voice hums a "mm-hmm" behind me. His chest is so close to my back, I can feel the vibrations of it, even if he's not touching me.

"Are you looking in to who did that to my sister? If she owed anyone anything?" My words waver in the air and I wish I could hold them steady. I wish I could sound as strong as I feel on my best of days. Not in this moment, not when I'm acutely aware that I'm whoring myself out to this arrogant bastard who could be using me, lying to me and toying with me just for his own sick pleasure. All so I can chase the ghost of whoever hurt my sister. Whoever took her from me.

"I already told you I was." His answer is clear and lacks the arrogance and dismissiveness he's given me so far today. I don't have to ask him to expand on his answer, since he does that himself. "Her death has caused ripple effects. When I have a name and a reason, you will too."

I can't help that I flinch when he lays a hand on my shoulder. I can't control the way I feel, and I struggle to hide that from him.

I'm so alone. In a room with this man I've been think-ing about for days, I feel so fucking alone. Maybe I made the memory of that night more than what was actually there.

I stare at the flames lingering among the pure white crystals. I let them mesmerize me and tell myself I don't have to go through with this. I don't have to rely on Jase Cross.

But the alternative crushes me; I can't risk never know-ing what happened and having to say goodbye without giv-ing her justice.

His left hand finds my hip and he rubs soothing cir-cles there over the sweater. Which only makes me hate him more until he lowers his lips to my ear and whispers, "Does it make a difference to you… if I admit I feel that chemistry too? That I have a desire to be near you?"

With a gentle kiss on my neck, that hard wall around me cracks and crumbles.

"It's no longer only business for me, cailín tine."

His words are a soothing balm. One I didn't realize I needed. My hand covers his, and I lean back into his chest, where he holds me. This man holds me because he wants to do just that. And I lean into him, because I want to do just that.

"I like it when you touch me," I whisper into the room, hoping it will keep my secret.

"And I like touching you," he says softly and runs the tip of his nose down the back of my neck, causing my eyes to close, my head to loll to the side and the pain to drift away slowly.

I don't want to be alone. I almost speak the realization aloud.

"I promise you, I will find out who hurt her." His words cause my eyes to open and when they do, I stare at the fire as Jase pulls my sweater over my head. It falls to the floor and then he whispers against the shell of my ear, "I will make them pay for what they did. And you will know every detail."

CHAPTER
15

Jase

WHEN SHE TURNS IN MY ARMS, I DON'T expect her to devour me with a kiss full of need and hunger. She can only hold up the hate routine for so long before her arms get weak and tired, and her body gives in to what it needs.

Pressing her lips to mine and spearing her fingers through my hair, she pulls me lower to her, standing on her tiptoes and holding her body against mine.

My tongue dives into her hot mouth, feeling the heat and need and lust she has to offer.

Her head falls back so she can breathe, deep and chaotically. I don't need air. I need to devour her.

With my arms wrapped around her and my lips traveling down her neck, down her bare shoulder, I take in every inch of her. Inhaling her sweet scent, memorizing the alluring sounds she lets slip from her lips. Dragging my teeth back up her neck, I hear her hiss my name, "Jase."

"Make me forget," she whimpers against my lips before I can ravage her.

Make me forget.

I don't speak the only response I can give her. *I will, if you do the same for me.*

Slamming my lips against hers, I grab her ass and lift her into my arms. Her legs straddle my waist as I carry her to the table.

Her hips need to be nestled against the padding, and the strap is meant to keep her in place. But I have no time for any of it. The urgency of our heated kiss fuels a primitive side of me with the need to have her under me as soon as possible.

With her heels digging into my ass, spurring me on, I groan in the hot air between us, "I need to be inside of you."

Her lips part, and I can almost hear her say the words. I know what she's going to say before she says it, *I need you too.*

But her gaze lingers, time pauses and the truth is lost in a haze of want and need.

Instead she kisses me, long and deep. Massaging my tongue and taking everything she wants with our kiss.

With her ass supported by the bench, I unbutton and unzip my jeans, letting them fall as I stroke my cock.

"I need you," she whispers into my mouth and then kisses me reverently again.

She's already wet, but so tight. Pushing two fingers inside of her, I stretch her until she can take three. "Your cunt was made for me to fuck," I tell her as I drag my knuckles against her front wall.

Her grip on the edge of the table nearly slips as her pussy spasms around my fingers.

I don't stop fucking her until her release is passed and her chest heaves for air and her face is flushed.

"Flip over," I command her but it's unneeded. I take the task on myself, gripping her hips and butting them against the bench.

Moving the head of my cock to her core, I press against her gently, not pushing in just yet.

A deep groan leaves me as I bend over her, my chest against her back. "You feel so fucking good," I whisper against her and just as she lifts her head to respond, I slam myself inside of her. Every inch of me in one swift stroke.

Her mouth drops open with a scream and her nails dig into the wood. Fuck, she's tight, so tight it almost hurts and I have to clench my jaw and force myself to slam into her over and over again.

Her small body jostles against the table and I know there will be bruises tomorrow. I'll be a happy man if she can't even walk.

A strangled noise leaves her as she gets impossibly tighter, cumming all over my cock.

"Jase," she moans my name, arching her back and scratching the wood as her body stiffens with her release.

With one hand on my shoulder, keeping her arched, and the other on her hip to pin her against the table, I ride through her release, taking her savagely and with no mercy.

It's more than just fucking her, this is about owning

154

her and I don't know when that happened.

She adjusts to me soon enough and my thrusts pick up, my balls drawing up with the need to release, but I can't give in just yet.

A desperate moan, loud and uncontrolled, fills the air. In an attempt to silence it, Beth covers her mouth with both hands as I thrust again and again.

"Don't you fucking dare." The words leave me at the same time that I grab her arms, pulling her hands away as I continue to fuck her with a ruthless pace.

Her upper body sways with every hard push of my hips against her ass.

"I want to hear every fucking sound." The words come out rough, from deep in my chest. "Scream for me."

CHAPTER
16

Jase

"I THINK I SHOULD LEAVE." BETHANY'S cadence is soft and innocent, and it doesn't hold any of the regret I'm sure she's feeling.

She's been silent since I brought her into the bedroom. Limp, well fucked, and sated.

And questioning everything.

I know the war that rages inside of her. I feel the same.

It's not just business. And there's no justification for the two of us being together.

She knows it. I know it. It's easy to get lost in each other's touch, but when it's over, what's left?

Beth turns in my bed, careful not to disturb the sheets to face me. Her small hand rests against my chest and I lift mine up to hers, holding her hand and bringing it to my lips so I can kiss her knuckles.

I don't know what this is. Or where it's going. All I know is that we shouldn't be doing it. She knows it too.

"Do you mind if I use your bathroom?" she asks, not even looking me in the eyes.

I nod, forcing her to peek up at me, and the well of emotion I'm feeling sinks deep into the soft browns and hints of green in her gaze.

I move to lie on my back as she scoots to the edge of the bed and quietly picks up her sweater from the pile of clothes we carried in from the den. I watch the dim light kiss the curves of her body until it's covered by the soft fabric.

Listening to her bare feet pad on the floor, then the flick of the light switch and the running water, I stare at the ceiling, knowing I need to give her an answer to her unspoken question, but the moment I do, I may lose her forever.

"You take medication?" Beth's question brings my attention to her as she stands in the threshold of the bathroom. One hand on the door, the other on a bottle of unmarked pills.

"No," I answer her, feeling the tension thicken.

Her weight shifts from one foot to the other. "So… you just keep your product in your bathroom then?" she dares to speak.

"My product?" I'm quick to throw off the covers and stalk toward her. My shoulders feel tense, hearing the confrontation in her voice. Maybe she just wants to pick a fight. Something she knows will end whatever it is between us and she can go back to pretending, *it's just business.* Bull-fucking-shit. I won't allow it.

"For a moment, I forgot. For a moment," she says under her breath, shutting the medicine cabinet. She turns around before I get to her and looks me in the eyes as she takes a step forward to meet me. "I was looking for Advil. And I thought..." She trails off and swallows hard, pulling her hair into a ponytail before continuing to speak. "For a moment, I forgot and I don't know how that's fucking possible."

I expect anger, but all I see in her features are disappointment and sadness. "Of course you have drugs here. You're a drug dealer."

Even as she stares at me, her eyes gloss over. She's so close to the edge of breaking. Looking for anything to push her over so she doesn't have to deal with the real cause of her pain.

Reaching around her, I open the medicine cabinet door and pull out the pills. "They're for sleeping," I tell her, and my voice comes out hard.

She tries to maneuver around me, but with my other hand, I grip her hip and keep her right there. "That's all they are. I don't do drugs and I don't like what I do, but I have to do it."

"You don't-"

My finger over her lips silences her. Her eyes spark and rage, but beneath the anger there's so much more.

"You don't have to understand." She pulls my hand away from her mouth just then.

"Yes, I do," she says and shakes her head. "You don't understand. I am not okay." Her last word cracks. "I don't know when I became this woman, or if I was always like this and never knew it because I was too busy solving someone else's problem. But right now, I have nothing." She swallows thickly, holding on to her strength. "I feel like my life is on the precipice of changing forever. And I don't want to go back to the girl I was, but I don't like where this is headed either. I don't have answers, and I need answers."

Her hand is still firmly gripping my wrist, and I stare at it until she loosens her hold.

"What answers do you need?"

My patience with her is higher than it should be. I'm softer and more willing to be gentle with her.

"I don't like what you do."

"That's not a question to be answered."

"Well I don't like it. I don't like that I like you."

I let her raised voice and condescension slide. For now. Only because it's true. She's only being honest, and I get it.

"Someone's going to do it, Bethany. There will always be someone in my position. You can't stop that. I can at least have control if I'm that someone."

"You sell drugs?" she asks, staring at the door to the bathroom before looking me in the eyes.

"You know I do. That answer isn't going to change."

"Why?"

"It's a long story," I say, keeping my voice firm.

"I have time."

"I don't want to tell it right now."

"Why are you making me pay Jenny's debt?" Her wide eyes beg me to give an answer that will calm her fears. I can see it clearly. "You didn't mention it when you came to the house. It wasn't until after you brought me here. And you don't need the money, that's for damn sure." Her gaze searches mine, looking for the only words she wants to hear.

"I wanted to let it go," I lie, hating myself for every word that comes out of me.

"How could she even owe so much? What did she use the money for?" she continues, not finding my answer satisfying enough.

Every question is another cut in the deepening gouge.

"You already got a question. Mine first." It's the only thing I can think of to hold her off for a moment. She quiets, watching me and waiting. Willing to give me whatever answer I need.

"How did you know about The Red Room? Why is that where you went to find answers?"

I already know the truth, so all while she speaks, I grasp for what answer I can give her in return.

"Jenny; she used to talk about it. The back room of The Red Room. All the time. I heard her on the phone."

"Who was she talking with?"

"I don't know." She's quick to add, "That's another question."

"Semantics."

"Answer my question!" Bethany pushes her hands into my chest. Not to hit me, not to push me, but to get my attention, to demand it. My blood simmers simply from her touch. "Why did she owe you so much money?"

"She owed it to Carter," I answer her, unable to deny her at this point. Blaming the debt on someone else like a coward. "He didn't want to let the debt go and be made to look like a fool."

"I don't understand what she did with all that money," she nearly whispers, looking past me as she searches through her memories for answers. Answers she'll never find.

"Debt adds up fast." I try to keep my tone gentle as I speak. "I can tell you I met her once," I add, and my confession brings her gaze to mine. "She was looking to buy that drug you just had."

"Sleeping pills?" She looks confused.

"Sweets is what they call it. Sweet Lullabies. We mostly use it for addicts to wean them off, put them out during their withdrawal." Bethany stares up at me, hanging on every word as I speak. I only wish this story had a better ending for her.

"She was strung out on coke; every telltale sign was there. And she was buying too much of the sweets. It didn't make sense. It wasn't for her. When we questioned her, she said it was for her brother. She left and never came around again."

"We don't have a brother."

"I know. We could tell she was lying to us, so we sent her away."

"That's what you know of my sister?" Shame and sadness lace her words.

"That's the only time I met her," I answer her and her gaze narrows, as if she can see through my truth to the lies I just told her moments ago. But this is the truth.

"I don't know who she was buying it for, or if it has anything to do with why she was killed."

I've lost a piece of her in this moment. I don't know how, but I did.

"Don't judge me, Beth. I'm the one who will pay for this."

She stares up at me, but she doesn't say a word. Still assessing everything I said, or maybe trying to see her sister as she was in her last days.

"You've got to calm down."

"I don't just calm down," she says, wrapping her arms around herself and I think she's done, but she tells me a story. "I was a preemie when I was born, and I almost died. My mother told me she thought it was God punishing her. She hadn't wanted my sister; she almost gave her up. Not that she was a bad person," she adds, quick to defend her mother. "She didn't think she'd be a good mom to her, and had broken up with my father just before she found out she was pregnant. She came very close to giving her up, but my father came back around and wanted to try to make things work. And then a few years later, they wanted to have me. And she told me she'd thought God was going to take me away. My lungs didn't work and the hospital couldn't do anything, so they put me in a helicopter and sent me away to a hospital that could save me. My mom couldn't come at first, because she lost a lot of blood.

"My grandfather used to say I came into this world fighting and I never stopped. He told me once, 'You'll leave this world fighting, Bethy. And I'll still be so proud of you.'" Tears cloud her eyes, but she doesn't shed them. Not my fiery girl; she holds on to every bit of her pain.

"It's okay," I tell her, rubbing her arm and then holding her when she falls into my chest.

"I'm sorry I'm a bitch," she tells me, sniffing away the last evidence that she may have been on the verge of crying.

"I don't know why I'm always ready to fight. I just am."

"It's okay, I already told you that."

"Why is it that when you say that, it feels like it really is?" The way she looks up at me in this moment is like I'm her hero. It's nothing but another lie.

"Because I'll do everything I can to make sure it is okay, maybe that's why?"

She sniffs once more and takes a step back to the counter as she says, "I should leave."

"I want you here. I don't want you to leave tonight."

"Why?" she asks. "Why do you want me to stay?"

"Do you really want to go to bed alone?"

"No," she whispers.

A moment passes between us. The look she gave me a moment ago is coming back.

"Jase, promise me one thing."

"What?"

"Don't hurt me."

I lie to her again, knowing that I hurt everyone I touch. Knowing I've already hurt her, although the truth of that hasn't revealed itself yet. "I won't hurt you," I tell her. I would have told her anything. Just to get her to stay.

CHAPTER
17

Bethany

ONE THING THE KIDS AT THE HOSPITAL DO all the time is lie. They lie about taking their medication. They lie about their symptoms. They lie for all sorts of reasons all the time.

It's my job to know when they're lying. I can't save them if I don't know the truth.

When Jase looked me in the eyes hours ago, he lied to me.

I don't know what piece of the conversation contained the lie. I don't know how much was a lie. I don't know why.

But I know he lied to me. And I can't let it go. The nagging thought won't let me sleep. He fucking lied to me. I put it all out there, allowed myself to be raw and vulnerable. My imperfect, broken, bitchy self. And he lied to my face. The worst part is that I'm sure it had to do with my sister.

That's what hurts the most.

Every minute that passed after seeing that look on his face when he lied, every minute I thought of how I could get it out of him. How I *needed* to get it out of him. How I was failing Jenny by letting it happen. How I was failing myself.

I'm careful as I slip off the sheet. I haven't slept at all, but he has. His breathing is even, and I listen to it as I gently climb out of the bed. My body is motionless when I stand up, listening to his inhales and exhales.

I already have my excuse ready in case he wakes. I never got that Advil, after all.

Every footstep is gentle as I move to the dresser, opening a drawer as silently as I can. The first drawer proves useless and as I shut it, Jase breathes in deeper, the pace of his breathing changing. I stand as still as I can, holding my own breath and praying he falls back asleep.

And he does. That steady, even breathing comes back.

With the rush of adrenaline fueling me, I move to his nightstand quietly, slowly, wondering if I've lost my fucking mind. I'm so close to him that he could reach out and grab me if he woke up. I watch his chest rise and fall as I open the drawer. The sound of it opening is soft, but noticeable. All the while, Jase sleeps.

I watch his chest for a steady rhythm; I watch his eyes for any movement. He's knocked the hell out.

The faint light from the room is enough to reflect off the metal of the set of cuffs. I only have two, but if I can get one wrapped around his wrist and linked to the bed, I'll have him where I need him.

Trapped, until he tells me the fucking truth.

I almost shut the drawer, almost, but then I realize he would be able to reach it, and nestled inside are both a gun and a knife.

The metal gleams in the night and I carefully pick up both weapons and move them to the top of the dresser on the other side of the room, away from his reach.

Thump. Thump. The heat of uneasiness creeps along my skin. My own breathing intensifies, my hands shake slightly and the metal of the handcuffs clinks in the quiet night.

Freezing where I am on the other side of the bed, I wait. And wait. Watching him carefully. If he woke up right now, I don't even know what he'd do to me.

But it's better to suffer that consequence than to accept him lying straight to my face, all the while, I fall for him … him and his lies.

It's what my mother did. She accepted my father's lies. And it left her a lonely woman. I won't be with a liar. I don't care about any debt or any other bullshit reason. I can't trust a liar.

I don't realize how angry I've become, not until Jase rolls over slightly in bed and my heart leaps up my throat.

The thought runs through my mind not to do it. That I'm out of my element and this world is more dangerous than I can handle. This isn't the person I am.

But he lied to me. …About Jenny.

Biting down on my bottom lip, I creep back up onto the bed and close one of the cuffs around an iron post of Jase's bed. There are four metal posts that surround his bed. The soft clink of the locks goes by slowly, *clink, clink, clink* and I swear he'll hear it, but his chest rises and falls evenly while he shows no signs of waking.

As I lean closer to him, closer to the other side, and ready to slip the other cuff through the post on that side of him, I gaze down at his face. In his sleep, he's still a man of power. But even with his strong stubbled jaw, there's a peacefulness I haven't seen.

He's only a man.

It fucking hurts to look at him. When someone can hurt you, it means you care. I have lived my life making sure not to care, so that I won't be hurt. And yet, Jase Cross pushed his way in, only to lie to me.

It solidifies my decision. I'll be damned either way.

Clink, clink, clink. With both handcuffs in place, I know securing the one on the left to his wrist will be easy. His wrist is close to the first cuff already. I'm sure he'll wake and then I'll be fucked, but I have to try. I'll have him where I want him.

With that thought, I go through with it, not second-guessing a thing.

I grab his wrist and it's by sheer dumb luck that he wakes up and grabs my throat with that hand. His dark eyes open wide and he stares daggers at me. Pinning me with a fierce look, the fear I knew I held for him deep down makes me still.

The look he shows is of startle and shock, and I don't let it distract me, even if I do scream out of instinct.

I drop my head down, shoving my face into the headboard, feeling the burn rising over my head from hitting my nose, and slip the metal around his wrist, scraping it against his skin as he screams at me, locking it into place.

"What the fuck are you doing?" his voice bellows in the room. His grip tightens for a moment, right before releasing me altogether.

I can still feel the imprint of his hand on my throat, the power he has to hurt me. I can feel it as I kick away from him, fighting with the sheets to get far enough away.

Scrambling backward, I fall hard off the bed onto my back, gasping for breath as my heart attempts to climb out of my throat.

Jase rips his arm back, yelling in vain as the metal digs into his wrist and the bed shakes, but he remains attached to it. Cuffed to the bed. He does it again and again and each time I lie on my back like a coward, my elbows propping me up on the floor as I wait with bated breath to see if I have trapped the beast.

"What the fuck did you do?" he jeers. "Where's the key?" he asks in a snarl.

Silence. *Did I really do it?* Thump.

"Where's the fucking key!" he screams until his face turns red. The anger seeps into the air around us as I slowly stand.

"I have the key," I manage to say somehow calmly, still in disbelief. He blinks the sleep from his eyes, breathing from his nostrils and slowly coming to the realization of what's happened. The way he looks down at me, like I betrayed him—I'd be a liar if I said it didn't kill something inside of me.

I ruin what I touch. I should have known this would end with him hating me.

"Give it to me," he requests with an eerily calm tone,

one that chills me to my bones.

"No," I say, and the word falls from me easily. More easily than I could have imagined as I stand up straighter, walking slowly around the edge of the bed. Not unlike the way he does to me when I undress for him.

His dark eyes narrow on me. "Don't do this. I won't be mad. Just give me the key."

Thump. Thump. Fear burns inside of me. The fear of both repenting, and the fear of going through with it.

I keep walking, slowly making my way to the dresser and Jase's eyes move to it before looking back at me. "What are you doing?" he asks me, and then I hear him swallow. I hear the hint of fear creeping into his voice. "Give me the key."

I ignore his demand and pick up the gun. I don't aim it at him, I merely hold it and tell him, "Put the open cuff around your other wrist." Although I lack true confidence, the gun slipping slightly in my sweaty palms.

"And how would you like me to do that?" Jase questions, a lack of patience and irritation are the only things I can hear in his voice. Like I'm a child asking for something ridiculous.

"You're a big boy," I bite back, "I'm sure you can figure it out."

All the while I watch him and he watches me, my heart does this pitter-patter in my chest making me think it's giving up on me as it stalls every time Jase looks back. Using the pillow and occasionally leaning down to hold the cuff between his teeth, he struggles to lock it. I don't trust him enough to do it myself though. There's no way he wouldn't grab me.

My heart beats faster with each passing second as he attempts to close the cuff himself.

Every moment his gaze touches mine, questioning why I'd do this, I question it myself.

"I don't want to hurt you," I whisper when I hear the cuff finally pushed into place. He rests his wrists against the iron rod, pushing it tighter and securing it.

"Then put the gun down," he urges me and I listen. I set it down on the dresser where it sat only minutes ago and hesitantly turn to him, each wrist cuffed to his bed.

"You can still uncuff me," he suggests with more dominance than he should have. Especially because I lift the knife at the end of his sentence.

"More cuffs." I speak the words and fight back the bile rising in my stomach from knowing my own intentions.

Jase's eyes stay on the knife as he answers me, "In the top drawer of the dresser. To the right side... with the ropes." His voice is dull and flat. "You're going to cuff my ankles?" he guesses correctly and I nod without looking at him, simply because I can't.

Thump. Thump. My heart feels like it's lagging behind as I pick up the cuffs from the drawer, right where he said they were.

"Why are you doing this?" he asks me; any hint of arrogance or even anger is gone.

I can barely swallow as I move toward him. With the sheet barely covering him but laid haphazardly over his groin still, the rest of him is fully exposed. He is Adonis. Trapped and furious, but ultimately mortal.

"I want answers," I say, and I don't know how I'm able to speak. "You lied to me. I know you did."

His only response is to stretch out his legs, not fighting, not resisting. Putting his ankles close to the rods.

He's helping me. Or it's a trick. I decide on the latter, moving closer, but hesitantly.

"Go on," he tells me, staring down at me.

I stand back far enough away from the footboard, cautious as I click the first cuff into place.

"Go ahead, cailín tine," he tells me, staring into my eyes. His nickname for me breaks my heart. Even as I look away, feeling shame and guilt consume me even though I know I have a good reason to do this. But it doesn't make it hurt any less.

With the last cuff in place, and Jase half sitting up in bed, leaning against the headboard and staring at me, I observe him from where I stand.

"What are you going to do now?" I ask him.

"Wait."

"You lied to me." I whisper the ragged words and turn the handle of the knife over in my hand.

"When?" he questions, and the muscles in his neck tighten.

A sad laugh leaves me and I'm only vaguely conscious of it when I hear it.

"So you did lie?" I ask weakly, feeling the weight against my chest. "And here I was hoping I was just crazy."

"I'd be hard-pressed in this moment to call you sane," Jase comments, and my eyes move to his. "Yes, I lied to you."

"What was a lie?" I ask him and take a step closer to the bed. The floorboard creaks under my step and I halt where I am, taking it as a warning.

"I don't want to tell you. It doesn't matter." He speaks a contradiction.

Wiping my forehead with the back of my hand, still holding the knife, I walk closer to him, gauging his ability to move, even though he's still as can be.

"I don't think you could do anything," I start to tell him as I stand right in front of the nightstand, "if I stand right here." Holding out my arm, I gently place the blade of the knife on his chest, not pushing at all, but letting him see how far away I can be while still capable of hurting him. "What do you think?" I ask him, wondering if I truly am crazy at this point.

"What do you want to know?" he asks, not answering my question.

"What did you lie about?"

"It's irrelevant."

"Anything relating to my sister is relevant." I grit out the words, pushing the knife down a little harder. Enough so the skin on his pec surrounding the knife, tightens under the blade.

"Did you hurt her?" The words come out unbidden.

"No, I told you that."

"And you told me you lied," I counter.

"I lied to protect you, Bethany." He almost says something else, but instead he rips his gaze away from me, gnashing his back teeth to keep him from talking.

Before I can continue, he tells me, "I have a name, but it's useless." His dark eyes lift to mine. "We think he got her hooked, intentionally or not, but he can't be tied to anything else. Nothing ties him to her death."

"Give me his name." The strong woman inside of me

applauds my efforts, rejoicing in the fact that it took this much to make him speak and that I was able to push myself to this point.

And that I have a name.

I have someone I can blame and punish, someone I can make pay for what they did to my sister. They tortured her. Broke her body. She was gone for so long, I don't know how long it went on. And then they burned her. They left nothing of her for me.

There will be nothing of them left when I find them.

"No." His answer dies in the tense air between us. It takes me a long moment to realize what he's even saying no to. My mind has gone to darker places, and tears streak down my cheek thinking about what she went through and that I wasn't there. I couldn't save her.

"Tell me who it was," I say as I move a bit closer, holding the knife with both hands, barely keeping it together. I let the tears fall with no restraint, and no conscious consent either. "I want his name!" I raise my voice and even to my own ears it sounds violent and uncontrolled.

Jase stares straight ahead, ignoring me, not answering.

"I don't want to hurt you." The confession sounds strangled.

"You don't have to," he answers.

"Give me the name, Jase!"

"You'll get yourself killed!" he yells back at me and the sound bellows from deep within him.

"You don't understand what they did to her!" I scream at him, feeling the well of emotion filling my lungs. I remember the fear when she went missing. "She would text me every day when she woke up, regardless of what time that ended up being. Sometimes she forgot. But every day, there was at least one text…" I trail off, remembering how angry I'd been when she messaged last. She wouldn't come back after I made her admit she had a problem. She refused to come back and get help. But she still messaged me every day. Until she didn't.

"And then there was nothing," I speak so softly, using what's left inside of me as the tears fall freely down my face.

"For days and then weeks, there was nothing but fear and hope. And fear is what won. Every day she didn't text me. The fear won." As I try to regain my composure, I wipe haphazardly at my face and focus on breathing.

"I waited in silence for nothing. The first forty-eight hours, no one did anything at all," I say and my words crack. "Why would they? She was reckless and headed down the wrong path."

The knife is still in my hands, still pressed to his skin when I tell him, "I knew something terrible had happened to her, and I could do nothing. She was still alive then. I know she was. I remember thinking that. That she was still out there. That I could feel her."

I'm brought back to my kitchen, crying on the floor, hating myself for pushing her away, regretting that I yelled at her, all alone and praying. Praying because God was the only one left to listen to me. Praying he could save her, because I couldn't.

"I had no name. No one had a name for me. But you do." I twist the knife just slightly, and suddenly feel it give, but I don't dare look. I don't look anywhere but into Jase's eyes, even as he seethes in pain.

"Give me the name."

"He'll kill you, Bethany." Sorrow etches his eyes and I know his answer already even before he says, "I won't do that."

I scream a wretched sound as I pull back the knife. It slices cleanly, so easily, leaving a bright red line in its path. Small and seemingly insignificant, but then blood pours from the wound and he bites back a sound of agony.

It's bright red. And it doesn't stop.

What have I done? Jase's intake is staggered but he doesn't show any other signs of pain.

"Fuck!" The word leaves me in a rush. "Jase," I say, and his name is a prayer on my lips. "No," I think out loud as my hand shakes and the knife drops to the floor. There's so much blood. There's so much soaking into the bed as it drips around his body.

It doesn't stop.

"Jase," I cry out his name as I ball up the bed sheets and press them to the laceration.

He breathes deep, staring at the ceiling. Silent, and ignoring me as I press more of the cotton linens to his chest, only for it to be soaked a half second later.

There's so much blood.

"I'm sorry," I utter as I rip the sheets out from under him, desperate to make it stop. "I'm so sorry."

The blood soaks through the fabric within seconds, staining my hands.

Staring down at the blood that lines the creases of my palms, I take a step back and then another.

What have I done?

CHAPTER
18

Jase

IT'S LIKE WHEN YOU WAKE UP FROM A NIGHTMARE. There's a moment where it all feels real and then, sometimes slowly, sometimes quickly, reality comes back to you. The horror stays, the damage done, the terrors in your sleep lingering as you walk down the steps of your quiet house to get a drink of water. And sometimes those monsters stand behind you. You can still sense them, even when you know they're not real.

That's what this feels like as the slice on my chest rips agony through my body. Like I can't get away from the ghosts in her eyes, even if she's woken from her dream. Even if disbelief and regret are all she feels, all she sees, all she recognizes.

The ghosts will still be there, waiting in the dark.

Every time she presses the sheets to the wound, a

renewed sense of pain spreads through my body, but I refuse to make a sound. My hands turn to fists and I pull against the cuffs, feeling the metal dig into my wrists.

"I'm so sorry. I don't... I didn't mean..." she says, choking on her words.

"I told you I would tell you," I remind her, flexing my wrists and breathing through the pain. I've had worse shit done to me. "When I know who it was, I will tell you and I will make them pay."

Besides, I fucking deserve this.

"I'm not going to give you a name without knowing for sure," I confess to her, letting her believe that's the only thing I've withheld, the only lie I've spoken. "I promise you."

Her beautiful hazel eyes lock onto mine, begging and pleading for forgiveness but more than that, an out. A way out of the nightmare she's in.

There's no way out of this shit though. This is what life is. It's what mourning is. A waking nightmare.

"I'm sorry," she blurts out before turning her back to me and running to the bathroom.

I hear her open the medicine cabinet and when I do, I push the escape lock on the cuffs with my thumb. It would be all too fucked up for her to have found the cuffs in my car; the ones I put on her, the ones I keep in my car. And not these safety cuffs I intend to use when I light her ass on fire with my paddle. The ones for play sold at sex shops.

Maybe I shouldn't have let it go on for as long as I did, but I think she needed this. She needed to get it out of her system.

I'm quiet as I unlock the ones on my ankles, taking my

time to put them away, gritting my teeth every time the sharp pain reminds me that she cut me.

With the drawer open, I drop the cuffs in, one by one when I hear her close the cabinet and I wait.

Her gasp is telling and I turn around slowly to see the halo of light surrounding her from the bathroom door. A bandage and gauze in one hand, and hydrogen peroxide in the other.

Horror plays in the depths of her eyes as she freezes where she is. She's a beautiful, broken mess.

I take a single step toward her; the floor groans and the only other sound is the hushed gasp she makes.

"Jase," she pleads, not hiding her fear. She doesn't hide anything; it's a big part of what I admire about her.

"Jase," she says again and this time my name is strangled as it leaves her. So much begging in only a single word as I take another step.

She trembles where she stands. I reach out for the bandages, and her arm drops dead to her side as she awaits her sentence. I place the bandage over the cut without sparing it a glance and wipe up the remaining blood with the gauze before tossing it behind her into the bathroom and onto the floor.

And she flinches from the movement. From my arm moving her way.

It fucking kills me. My chest doesn't feel a goddamn thing from the cut. But it feels everything knowing that she thought I was going to hit her. That I would strike her.

Everyone deserves punishment for their sins. And I accept mine. But I won't accept losing her.

Her eyes never leave mine, and mine never leave hers.

She doesn't beg for mercy; she doesn't try to run.

The world is full of broken birds and pain. I won't add to it.

Not her. Not my fiery girl, my *cailín tine*.

"Jase." She says my name thickly and swallows after a second passes of silence. Just the two of us knowing the other's pain, knowing what's happened wasn't a nightmare, it was real.

"I'm sor-"

I cut her off with my own apology. "I'm sorry I can't bring her back." The emotion wells in my throat as I add, "If I could, if I had that power, I wouldn't be feeling the same shit you are."

The tense air changes, and everything falls around us. For me it does. Nothing else exists for me but her.

"If I could, I would," I tell her as I brush her hair off her shoulder and lower my lips to hers. It's all done slowly. I'll be sweet with her tonight.

Her lips brush against mine gently and then she deepens our kiss.

Her fingers are hesitant at first, as if she's still expecting me to snap like she did.

I have all the time in the world for her tonight. To see what's really here. To know what's between us.

I can show her, and I do. Slowly, gently, and with every small touch, I chip away at any armor she has.

I don't want the hate; I don't want the fight.

Not tonight.

Tonight I make her feel loved.

A part of me knows it's selfish, because I don't deserve her or any of this. But tonight I need to feel loved too.

CHAPTER
19

Bethany

The Coverless Book
Fourth Chapter

"Do you think Mama will be okay with it?" I ask Caroline, nervously peeking up at her. The silk is like water under my fingers. So smooth and easily flowing. "I've never worn anything like it."

"It's perfect for your first date," Caroline tells me with that sweet Southern charm.

I turn around fully to face her, repeating my question, "But do you think Mama will be okay with it?"

Caroline's expression falters.

"I think your mama would love it, Emmy," Caroline says, forcing that false smile to her lips. She's worked for our family since just before I got sick. I know all her tells and

that smile she's plastered on her face is only there to hide the truth. She hates my mother, but I don't know why.

"She's sick too," I whisper defensively. "That's why she's not here." The excuse falls flat, just like it does every time.

"She's not sick like you. She's just in pain," Miss Caroline corrects me.

Those in the most pain, cause pain. My mother told me that once. It was a while ago and she said that's why she doesn't see me very much. She doesn't want to hurt me. I know it kills her inside to know what's happening to me. "Pain is a sickness, isn't it?" I ask Caroline.

The false smile wavers as she reaches down to pick up the pair of shoes. "Your first pair of heels," she states and pretends she didn't hear me. She does that sometimes. She doesn't answer me when I ask questions. I know they're insignificant, but I have no one else to talk to. Some days I wonder if I've spoken when she does that.

I only know I have when I hear her sniffle. They don't like to see me like this, frail and losing weight and muscle like I am. No one does. I'm not just sick; I'm dying. That's what the doctors say.

Smoothing the ruby red silk fabric with my hand, I turn to the mirror thinking, Jake will like me in this dress. He won't mind seeing me sick. He doesn't cry when I tell him I'm invincible, not like Mama and not like Miss Caroline.

Jake thinks I'm pretty. He thinks I'm sweet.

"Soup, Emmy," Caroline calls out and I can hear the spoon clinking against the porcelain.

"Is it- "

Before I can finish, Miss Caroline nods and says, "Of course it is. I had to make your favorite for today. Drink up, baby, you need to be strong."

"*I already am strong,*" *I tell her with a smile, feeling the excitement of tonight. "Haven't I told you? I'm invincible."*

The story grips me as the pages turn. A young boy and a sick girl, falling in love even though they know it won't last. I can't help but to think it's not that simple. I hate her mother and I like Miss Caroline, but I feel sorry for Emmy. It's funny how they feel so real when I curl up under the blanket and let the night disappear in between the pages of The Coverless Book.

Lines of a dark blue ink run along the pages. And with every line, I add it to the list in my notepad.

I'm invincible.

Those in the most pain, cause pain.

I don't feel sick when he looks at me like that; I can only feel cherished with his gaze on me.

Agony is meaningless; only love can relate.

There is no pattern. No reason to think there's a hidden message lying inside. But I do. I can't help but to hope that I'm missing something. Anything. I just want my sister to tell me something.

Or at least I did. Days ago.

Before that night with Jase. The night everything changed. Somehow, he took my fight away, but with it, there's relief.

It's been two days and he hasn't messaged me, and I haven't messaged him either.

I don't know how it happened, but everything feels

different now.

With every thrust against his bedroom wall, he forced the air from my lungs. He took it, he made it his. The air, my body... and more.

Forgiveness and understanding can do something to a person. Especially when you don't feel worthy of it.

When I stepped out of that bathroom, not knowing what the hell I was going to do or what the hell I was thinking when I cuffed him, I wouldn't have fathomed he'd be there facing me.

What did I think would happen even if I did get a name from him?

That somehow he would let me out of his gilded cage after he admitted what he lied about? That he wouldn't hold it against me that I'd cuffed him up and threatened him?

I don't know what the hell I was thinking. I've never been sorrier for hurting someone. I can't believe I did that.

There will be consequences, I remember Jase's words last night. Just before I fell asleep, he told me the night wasn't forgiven wholly, until there were consequences.

And I accept it. Whatever those consequences may be.

I don't know what happened to make me think I could, and that I should, lay a knife to his skin.

The only way I can justify it, is that I think it happened for a reason.

I think we were meant to have that moment. The moment when he kissed me, and he made it feel okay to let go. He made me feel like if I was with him, everything would be the way it should be.

He made me feel like I wasn't as broken as I thought I was.

And I gave him everything I had to give. Even if it's not much.

I would give him everything and anything from this day forward.

His forgiveness and touch are worth more than I'll ever have.

Ping. My phone goes off with a text message, followed by another.

Are you okay?

How are you feeling?

Two different texts, from two different people. And I'm grateful for the distraction.

One's from Laura and one's from Jase.

I'm feeling good, how are you? I text them both the same thing. I don't even realize it at first.

I just haven't heard from you. Anything new? Laura writes back first.

I write a few words and delete them. Write some more and delete those too. I finally settle on, *Maybe. I'll know more when we go out this weekend.*

My heart does this little pitter-patter thing and my head tells it that it's naïve.

The three dots at the bottom left of the screen tell me she's writing something, but before she can finish, Jase messages.

I was hoping to see you tonight. But things came up. Tomorrow.

He doesn't ask. He tells.

I debate on what to say, focusing on the first part and then the second. *He was hoping to see me.* The butterflies Emmy feels ... I feel them too. They kind of scare me.

Everything that's happening scares me.

Before I can respond to him, Laura writes back.

What's new? I can't take the suspense. You know I thrive on instant gratification.

Shifting on the sofa, I pull the blanket up my lap, hating the draft coming from the old window and focusing on that rather than the butterflies.

I pick up my mug and take a swig of it; the decaf tea is lukewarm, but still satisfying.

I don't know exactly what it is yet, I tell Laura. *But when I do, I'll let you know.*

I press send and then realize I sent it to the wrong fucking person. The mug slams down onto the table when I realize, but thankfully my tea's almost gone so none of it splashes out.

"Fuck, fuck, fuck, fuck," I mutter under my breath, feeling my heart race.

Sorry, I meant that for someone else. See you tomorrow. I type out the response quickly, before Jase can respond. My heart's a damn war drum as I copy and paste what I sent him to send to Laura.

"Fuck a duck," I say out loud, letting my head fall back on the sofa. I am … a mess. A living, breathing mess.

Omg that's so exciting! Tell me everything! Laura writes immediately.

You don't know what "what" is? What is "what?" And who are you talking to? Jase writes back. Fuck, he knows. It doesn't take a genius to know what I'm talking about.

"Shit, shit, shit," is all I can think and say as I stare at his message.

Rubbing the stress away from my forehead, I decide

they can get the same message again.

I'm heading to bed. Sorry, we'll talk later. As soon as the text is sent, I toss the phone on the other side of the sofa and stare at it as it goes off. Again and again. Taunting me every time. And with each one, I wonder if it's Jase, or Laura.

Fuck both of those conversations. It's late, and I'm obviously not with it. I'm tired, but I haven't been able to sleep. They can wait. Everything can wait.

Rubbing my eyes, and ignoring the sick feeling I have inside, I finally get up off the sofa and wonder if I should grab another cup of tea, or just pass out like I said I was going to do.

My mind won't stop with all the questions though. So sleeping is nonexistent.

I don't know what we are. Jase and me. I don't know where this is going. And I don't know how I'll be all right if I don't have Jase in my life. I owe him a debt, and the hours are numbered. It will come to an end. I'm fully aware of that, and it's terrifying.

Sleep doesn't come easy for me and with that thought in mind, I pick up the small bottle of pills from my purse. The handwriting on the back merely says, *All you need is one.*

I can add assault and theft to my résumé after what happened two nights ago.

Before I left Jase's home, I swiped the bottle of sleeping pills from his medicine cabinet. I don't know if he knows yet, or what he'll do when he finds out, but he can add them to my tab.

This goes against everything I know; everything I've

ever done. Both the stealing and taking the drugs. *They're only sleeping pills*, I remind myself. And I desperately need sleep. Holding the pill up, I see it's a gel capsule with liquid inside. Just like an Advil.

But everything about this week is more than morally ambiguous. And everything has changed.

The phone pings again and I check to see what they said after getting a glass of water and a single pill.

Laura wrote back a novel. Text after text demanding I give her every detail. To which I reply, *I still love you! I'll tell you all of it soon!*

And Jase wrote back, *Sleep well.* To which I reply, *You too.* And feel far too much just from being able to tell him goodnight.

⌒⌒⌒

It's so cold here. At first I don't know where I am. Sleep came too easily. I remember feeling my entire body lift as if I'd become weightless, right before falling so deeply into darkness. Even now I can remember it, as if I could touch it and relive it. Although I know it's already passed.

I fell and fell, but it didn't feel like falling. Everything else was moving around me until I landed in this room. A small room with dirty white walls. There's a radiator in the corner with a thick coat of paint, or maybe many coats of paint. It's white too, like the walls. The thin wooden boards on the floor are old and they don't like me walking across them. They tell me I don't belong here. They tell me to go back.

But I hear the ripping.

Something is being torn behind the old chair. It's a tufted chair, and maybe it was once expensive, but faded fabric is being torn down the back of it.

Rip, another tear and I hear something else. The sound of a muffled sob. A shuddered breath and the sound of gentle rocking. Just behind the chair.

I take another step, and a freezing prick dances along every inch of my skin. It's so cold it hurts, like an ice pick stabbing me everywhere.

It doesn't matter though. Nothing does. Because I see her.

She's there, Jenny's there. Sitting cross-legged on the floor, rocking back and forth with a book in her hand. The Coverless Book.

"Jenny," I cry out her name and try to go to her, but the chair doesn't let me; its torn fabric holds me where I am, making a vine around my ankles. My upper body tumbles forward, falling onto the back of the chair. "Jenny!" I scream as I reach out to her. But I can't reach her, and she can't hear me.

Her hair is so dirty, long and stringy now. The tears on my cheek turn to ice.

"Jenny," I whisper, but her name is lost in the cold air as I try to move from where I am. How is it holding me back? Let me go! She's my sister! She's here!

I fight against it all, but my hips are now tied down as well. I can't move to her; I can't even feel my legs. Please, let me go. I have to go to her!

The book falls, and the sound whips my eyes to her once again as Jenny covers her face to cry. Her arm has a mark-ing, is it a quote? A tattoo?

What is it?

Her shoulders shake as tears stream down her cheeks

and I tell her not to cry. I tell her it's okay, that I'm here. Her wide, dark eyes look up at me. Her pale skin is nearly as white as the fog from her breath.

It's so cold here.

"You shouldn't be here," she says, staring straight into my eyes. Both pain and chills consume me.

"Come with me," I beg her, licking my chapped lips and I swear ice coats them after. "Come with me, Jenny!" I scream, feeling the bite of a chill deep in my lungs, and she only tilts her head as if she doesn't understand.

The torturous feeling of being trapped makes me scream a wretched cry. And Jenny only stares at me.

"I just wanted them to be okay," she tells me as if she's apologizing. "Someone needs to be okay."

"Who?" I beg her for an answer. "Who did this to you? Where are you?"

Her voice cracks and she tells me repeatedly, "You shouldn't be here." Over and over in the same way, all while she shakes her head and rocks. "You shouldn't be here."

Darkness descends, like a storm brewing inside of the small room. "Jenny, come with me!" I scream again, "Jenny, come with me!" as the room stretches, tearing her away from me. No!

"Don't believe them," she whispers and I hear it as if she's next to me. As if she's whispered it into my ear.

"Don't believe the lies. They'll all tell you lies."

Even when she's gone and there's only darkness left, she tells me, "Don't believe your heart; it lies to you too."

CHAPTER
20

Jase

"WHAT HAPPENED?" I ASK HER THE second I shut her front door. I've only just gotten here, intent on implementing consequences, and I'm already changing my mind.

Her eyes are bloodshot, and her skin is pale. Hugging her knees into her chest, she's seated on her sofa, staring at nothing.

"Nothing," she's quick to tell me. "I didn't think you'd be here in the morning. I thought you'd come at night," she adds and then wipes under her eyes as she tosses the blanket to the side of the sofa.

"I don't like it when I ask a question and you lie to me," I speak as I walk into the living room. Not a single light is on and the curtains are shut tight. It's too dark.

That gets her attention, and a hint of the girl I know

shows herself when she answers smartly, "Oh, it's not the best feeling, is it?"

The sarcastic response leaves her easily, and she watches me as I narrow my gaze at her. From bad to worse, the air changes.

"Something happened from the time you left me to just now." I speak clearly, with no room for argument and Beth crosses her arms, staring just past me for a moment before looking me in the eyes.

She's in nothing but a sleepshirt that's rumpled, and dark circles are present under her eyes. Even still, she's beautiful, the kind of beautiful I want to hold on to.

"Are you going to tell me?" I ask her, not breaking our stare.

Time ticks by and I think she's going to keep it from me, but finally she looks to the kitchen and then back at me. "Over coffee," she tells me.

She turns toward the kitchen like she's going to walk there, but then pauses and looks over her shoulder. "You coming?" she asks, and I follow. Watching every detail, noticing the way her movements lag, the way she sniffs after a long exhale, like she's been crying. The way she leans against the counter after putting the coffee grinds in the pot, like she can barely stand on her own.

"What the fuck happened?" I ask her and lean against her refrigerator. Standing across from her, we're only feet apart but it feels like so much farther away. I should know everything that happens. I'll correct that mistake immediately.

"Where do we stand on the debt?" she asks and then clears her throat as the coffee machine rumbles to life.

"I wrote it down; don't have it with me." I give her a bullshit answer and ask again, but harder this time, "What happened?"

Lifting up her head to look me in the eyes, her lips pull down and she tells me in a tight voice, "I wasn't sleeping... not at all since Jenny..." She leaves the remainder unspoken. "So I took those pills you had." She crosses her arms, looking down at the coffee pot and licking her lower lip before telling me, "I'm sorry. It was shitty of me and I don't know why I'm doing so many shitty things, to be honest."

Her arms unfold and she rests her elbows on the counter, like she's talking to the coffee pot instead of me. Her fingers graze her hairline as she keeps going. "That drug doesn't work; I'll tell you that." As she speaks her voice is dampened, although she tries to keep it even. "I had the most awful dream, but it felt so real." I take a tentative step forward, getting closer to her, but am careful to keep far enough back so she won't feel threatened.

She reminds me of a caged animal backed into a corner. One who's given up and given in, but still frightened and not ashamed to admit it. One who would still try to hurt you, and you'd be the one to blame, because it warned you so.

"It was so real, Jase," she whispers and before I can ask what her dream was, she tells me. "Jenny was there, ripping the cover off the book." She turns around to face what little of the living room she can see from this angle. Her hand falls to her side as she peeks up at me.

A deep well of emotions burns in her gaze, enrapturing me and refusing to let me go. "She said I didn't belong there and she wouldn't come back with me." She has to

192

whisper her words, her voice is so fragile. Like she really believed it happened.

"I'm sorry I stole from you, and I'm sorry I even took it. I don't know what's happening to me." Bringing the heels of her hands up to her cheeks she wipes at the stray tears and that's when I hold her, rocking her in my arms and shushing her.

"I hate crying... why am I crying?" Her frustration shows as she holds on to the pain, still not having learned to let it go.

The coffee pot stops, and I can't hear anything. She's stiff in my arms, not crying, but not getting better either.

She's stuck in that moment. The monster in her dreams, following in her shadows.

"You want to go upstairs?"

She doesn't answer right away and I add, "You need to sleep."

It takes a moment, it always does with her, ever defiant, but she nods eventually. She pushes off from the counter, leaving the black coffee to steam in the mug where it sits, knowing it'll go untouched and turn cold.

Her arms stay wrapped around her as she walks up the old stairs, and I follow behind her, listening to the wooden steps creak with every few steps.

I keep a hand splayed on her back and when we make it to the bedroom, she stops outside of the door. "You don't have to babysit me," she tells me, craning her neck to look up at me in the dimly lit hall.

"Maybe I want to lie in bed with you, ever think of that?" I ask her softly, letting the back of my fingers brush her cheek.

She takes my hand in both of hers and opens the door to her bedroom. It's smaller than mine, but nice. Her dresser looks older, maybe an antique like the vanity she has in the corner of her room.

Everything is neatly in place, not a single piece of clothing is out, nothing is askew. Nothing except for the bed. It looks like she just got out of it. The top sheet's a tangled mess and the down comforter is still wrapped up like a cocoon.

"When did you get up?" I ask her.

She shrugs and pulls back the blankets, fixing them as she answers, "I think around three... I don't remember."

"It was almost midnight when you said you were going to bed."

"Yes," is all she answers me.

"Come here." I rip her away from straightening the sheets to hold her, and she clings to me. "It wasn't real," I whisper in her hair.

"I wish..." she pauses, then swallows thickly before confessing, "I wish it was in some way, because at least I got to see her."

Her shoulders shudder in my arms. I don't have words to answer her, so I lay her in bed, helping her with the blankets and climbing in next to her.

The kisses start with the intent to soothe her pain. Letting my lips kiss her jaw, where the tearstains are. Up her neck, to make her feel more.

And she does, she breathes out heavily, keeping her eyes closed and letting her hands linger down my body.

Slowly it turns to more. She deepens the kisses. She holds me closer and demands more.

"You're still in trouble," I whisper against her lips, reminding her that she needs to be punished. Her response is merely a moan as she continues to devour me with her touch.

"Not tonight, but it's coming."

Her eyes open slowly, staring into mine and she whispers, "I know."

"Tell me what you want." I give her the one demand, wanting her to control this. Giving her something I haven't before.

"Don't make this harder on me. Please," she begs me and I nearly turn her onto her belly, to fuck her into the mattress like I've wanted to do since the day I first laid eyes on her, but then she says, "I don't want to beg you for something like... like..."

"Like what?" I ask, not following.

"I don't want to consciously ask... for... for this," she whispers and opens her eyes to look back at me.

It takes a long moment to feel how deep that cut me. Maybe it's the disbelief. "To ask for something ... like for me to fuck you?" My tone doesn't hide a damn thing I'm feeling as I sit up straighter in bed. "Is it offensive? Or do you just not want to admit that you want me?"

"Jase." Bethany wakes in this moment, her eyes more alive than they were downstairs. Brushing the hair out of her face, she sits up straighter, and blinks away the haze of lust.

"Tell me what you want." I give her the request again. Waiting. Every second the fucking agony grows deeper and deeper.

"Jase," she pleads with me. But I ask for so little now.

I'm trying to give her everything to make it right, but I need this. "Tell me," I say. The demand comes out hard and her expression falls.

A moment passes and she takes my hand, but her grip is weak.

"Please," she begs me, "I don't want to be alone."

"I know that, but you don't want to be with me either. Do you? We shouldn't be doing this anyway." I say the words without thinking. I know we've both thought it. That what this is today isn't what it was that night I had her sign the contract. And two nights ago, we should have parted ways. It's volatile and wrong. Being with her is going to be my downfall, I already know it.

And yet here I am waiting for her answer, because she's the only one of the two of us who has the balls to admit out loud that we shouldn't be together.

She hesitates, although she doesn't deny it. She doesn't say anything. The silence grows between us, separating us and making it seem as if the last time we were together never happened.

Thump, there's the dull pain in my chest. It flourishes inside of me as I stand there in silence.

"After what I did for you, I deserve better than that," I snap back. It fucking hurts. There's a splintering sensation in my chest as if the absence of her words truly injured me more than that cut she gave me the other night. Only one will scar.

Her lips turn down as she swallows, making her throat tight. Her inhale quivers but instead of saying anything, she shakes her head, her hair sweeping around her shoulders as she looks away.

Nothing. She gives me nothing and with that I turn my back to her, slamming the door shut behind me. As hard as I can. The force of it travels up my arm, lingering as I walk away from her.

I could tell her she still owes me; I could tell her that. But right now, I don't want to.

An awful sound travels down the hall, following me. A sob she tries to cover. The kind you hope comes out silent, but it's ragged and fierce. My footsteps thunder behind me as I take the stairs as quickly as I can.

The kind of sobs that you can't control. The kind that hurt.

Both the pounding of my shoes as I leave and the evidence of her misery, both are uncontrolled and painful.

I have seen so much brokenness in my short life. I hate it. I hate how easily everything can be destroyed and wasted. It's so useless to live day by day, not just seeing it all around you, but making it so.

Standing at the bottom of her stairs, with one hand on the wall and the other gripping the banister, I listen to her cry. Crying for me? And the pain she's caused me? Crying for herself and how alone and empty her life truly is? Crying for us?

And it takes me back to the time I heard similar cries. A time I left.

And I remember what was left of me when I came back to see the damage done.

My body tenses and my throat dries as I stand in between the man I was before and the man I'll be tomorrow.

Tonight is mine regardless and knowing that, I turn on my heels and make my way back up the stairs as quickly as

I can, pushing her door open without knocking. Her wide eyes fly to mine as I kick the door shut behind me.

"Jase?" She whispers my name in the same way the snow falls around us. Gentle and hopeful the fall won't last for long.

She moves on the bed, making a spot for me easily enough although her eyes are still wide and searching for answers. She stays sitting up even though I climb in and lie down back where I was, pulling the covers over my clothes.

It's too hot, but it's better than taking the time to do something other than lie down with her.

Patting the bed, I tell her to lie down, noting how gruff my voice is. How raw.

"Are you angry?" she asks and I tell her I've always been.

Molding her small body to mine, she rests her hands on my chest, still wary, still exhausted. Still hoping for more. "I'm sorry," she whispers and I tell her so am I.

Hope is a long way of saying goodbye. Even I know that.

Her hair tickles my nose when I kiss the crown of her head. The covers rustle as I move my arm around her, rubbing soothing circles on her back.

Time marches on and with it the memories of long ago play in my mind. Making me regretful. Making me question everything.

"Why did you come back?" she asks me before brushing her cheek against my chest and planting a small kiss in the dip just beneath my throat.

I confess a truth she could use against me. Even knowing that, still I admit, "I don't want you to be alone either."

CHAPTER
21

Jase

THE SNOW'S FALLING. IT'S ONLY A LIGHT dusting, but it decided to come right this moment, right as my brother leads his love across the cemetery.

One grave has been there for half her life. The one next to it has freshly upturned dirt. The snow covers each of the graves equally as Aria silently mourns, her body shaking slightly against Carter's chest.

I spoke to her father only days before he met his death. A death he knew was coming. A death that always comes for men like us.

The powerful man asked me to find a way. Swallowing his pride when he thought his daughter was going to die because of him.

Talvery wasn't ready to lose his daughter. She swears

he was going to kill her.

That's the irony in it all.

He was a bad man. And that's the crux of the problem. She expected him to do bad things, even if she loved him in his last days, although I don't believe she did love him anymore.

She swears he was going to shoot her, but there was only one gun cocked and it wasn't her father's. She heard it, she speaks of it, but she doesn't realize what really happened and I don't have the heart to tell her.

The man who pulled the trigger confessed to me. He said in the old man's last breaths, he laid down his gun and said goodbye to his daughter. But she didn't see, clinging to a man she loved and not to the man who gave up fighting to ensure she would be loved one more day.

That's what this life brings. A twisted love of betrayal. A reality that is unjust and riddled with deceit.

Aria lays a single rose across her mother's grave, but not her father's, even though when he called me, he said he would give up everything right then and there, if I promised we'd keep her safe.

There was no negotiation we could offer.

Her father had to die. And Aria was never in harm's way. The man had nothing to barter with, not when he knew we'd take it all. I never told Carter. And I never will. The perception that her father was a ruthless crime lord past his date of redemption is what makes it okay. It makes it righteous that she only lays a rose down for her mother, a woman who betrayed everyone to benefit herself.

Watching Carter hold her hand, kiss her hair and comfort her, only reminds me of what could have been. If the gun cocked had been Talvery's and my brother was in that grave instead.

Bright lights reflect a section of falling snow. Headlights from a cop car pulling in across the parking lot I'm sitting in.

Gripping the steering wheel tighter, I take into account everyone here. It's only me, still in the driver's seat waiting for Carter to bring Aria back and the sole cop parking his vehicle across from mine.

Before Carter has a chance to look behind him, taking attention away from Aria, I message him. *I've got it. Stay with her.*

A second passes, and another before Carter looks down at the message, back at me, and then to the cop, who opens his door in that moment.

Officer Walsh.

The sound of his door closing echoes in the vacant air. It's hollow and reflects its own surroundings.

As I open my car door, welcoming the cold air, breathing it in and letting it bite across my skin, I nod at Carter, who nods in return, holding Aria closer, but not making a move to leave.

The snow crunches beneath my shoes, soft and gentle as it falls. It vanishes beneath my footprints as I make my way around to the front of my car, leaning against it and waiting for him.

As I take in the officer, a crooked smile forms on my face. We're wearing the same coat. A dark gray wool blend. "Nice coat, Officer Walsh," I greet him and offer a hand. He's hesitant to accept, but he does.

Meeting him toe to toe, eye to eye, his grip is strong.

"So you've heard of me?" he asks. I lick my lower lip, looking over my shoulder to check on Carter one more time before I answer him, "I heard someone was asking about me, someone who fit your description."

"Funny," he answers with a hint of humor in his voice, although his pale blue eyes are only assessing. "I heard the same about you."

"That I was asking about you?" I ask with feigned shock as I bring my thumb up to point back at me. "I only asked who was asking about me and my club."

"The Red Room." The officer's voice lowers and his gaze narrows as he speaks. He slips his hands into his coat pockets and I wait for more, simply nodding at his words.

Some cops are easy to pay off. They need money, they want power, or even just to feel like they're high on life and fitting into a world they could only dream of running themselves.

I can spot them easily. The way they walk, talk—shit, even the clothes they wear on their time off. It's all so fucking obvious. The only question that needs answering is: how much do I need to pay them until they're in my back pocket?

Not Cody Walsh.

"What is it that you want, Officer?" I ask him and then add, "Anything I can help you with?"

"Anything you had in mind?" he asks in return, tilting his chin back and waiting.

The smirk on my face grows. "I don't dislike having conversations with cops." I follow his previous gaze just as he looks back at me and see Carter and Aria making their way back to the car that's still running. "But I don't really like to start a conversation either."

He's playing me. Thinking I'll try to bribe him for nothing. What a fucking prick.

"Is that his wife?" he asks me, and I tell him the truth. "His fiancée."

"Aria Talvery," he comments.

"You know a lot of names for being new around here."

"It's my job," he answers defensively.

"Is it?" I rock back on my shoes as I slip my hands into my pockets. My warm breath turns to fog in the air. "You know everyone's name who you pull over then?" I ask him.

"Not unless their name is in the file of the case I'm working on."

"A case?" I ask him as the cold air runs over my skin, seeping through my muscles and deep down into the marrow of my bones. I feel the shards of ice everywhere, but I don't show it. "It's the first time I'm hearing about a case."

"A house burned down, killing over a dozen men, explosives."

"Aria's family home," I remark, acknowledging him with a nod. "What a tragedy."

"It was arson, and one of a string of violent crimes that leads back to you and your brothers."

With the sound of the car door opening behind me, indicating Carter is helping Aria into the backseat, my patience is gone.

"If you have questions, you can ask my lawyer."

"I don't have any for you," he tells me and I huff a humorless laugh before responding, "Then why come to pay this visit?"

"I wanted to see her reaction; if she was remorseful at all."

"Aria?" The shock is apparent in my tone and my expression, because I didn't hide it in the least. I shouldn't be speaking her name. I shouldn't even engage with this fucker. And that's the only reason I'm silent when he adds, "Knowing she's sleeping with her father's killer..."

He shakes his head, although his eyes never leave mine.

"Is that all then?" I ask him.

A moment passes, and with it comes a gust of cold wind. Each day's been more bitter than the last and with a snowstorm coming, the worst is yet to come.

"That's all," he says and then his eyes drift to my windshield before he adds, "And pay your parking tickets. Wouldn't want that to be what gets you."

All I give him is a short wave, right before snatching a small piece of paper off the windshield. It's not a parking ticket, it's a thick piece of yellow paper folded in half. It's been here for a while, partially covered by the snow. And knowing that, I look back to see if Walsh is watching. His eyes are on Carter, not me. Thank fuck.

I don't know who the fuck left it, but I'm not going to figure that out while under the watchful eyes of Officer Walsh.

Lacking any emotion at all, I bid the man farewell. "Have a good night, Officer."

With my back to Walsh I share a glance with Carter, who's waiting by the backseat door on the driver's side, one hand on the handle, his other hand in his pocket.

"You too," the officer calls out in the bitterly cold air,

already making his way back to his car.

It's silent when I close the door. Aria tries to speak, but I hear Carter shush her, telling her to wait for the officer to leave. Peeking at her in the rearview mirror, worry clouds her tired eyes.

"Everything's fine," Carter reassures her and she lays her cheek, bright red from the frigid air, onto his shoulder.

My gaze moves from the cop car, reversing out of the spot, to the note. The sound of the thick paper opening is all I pay attention to as Officer Walsh drives away, leaving us alone in the parking lot.

A sharp ringing in my ear accompanies my slow breaths and the freezing sensation that takes over when I glance at the note, a script font I recognize as Marcus's.

How the fuck did he leave a note? And when? I read his message and then read it again. The psychopath speaks in riddles.

You took my pawn. I have another.
The game hasn't stopped. It's only changed slightly.
Just remember, the king can only hope to be a pawn when his queen is gone.

Every hair on my body stands on end after reading the note, knowing he was here. How the fuck did I not see him?

"What's wrong?" Carter asks me as I reach for my phone, needing to tell Seth and everyone else what happened and get security footage immediately.

But Seth's already texted me.

And I sit there motionless in my seat, reading what he

wrote as Carter bites out my name, demanding an answer I don't have to give.

We found the sister.
She's alive.
Marcus has her.

CHAPTER
22

Bethany

I CAN'T STOP READING. WHEN I DO, I HAVE TO face reality and I'm not ready to face the consequences of my decisions yet. I'd rather get lost in the pages.

Every time they kiss, I think of Jase Cross.

I think I love him.

I love my enemy.

Why couldn't I be like the characters in this book? Why couldn't I be like Emmy and fall for the boy who loves her just as much and the only thing they have keeping them apart, is whether or not they're both still breathing?

Why did I have to fall for a villain? Maybe that's what I deserve. Deep down inside though, I don't think I even deserve him.

Books are a portal to another world, but they lead to other places too. To places deep inside you still filled with hope and a desperate need for love. Places where your loneliness doesn't exist, because you know how it can be filled.

Jase isn't a good man, but he's not a bad one either. I refuse to believe it. He's a damaged man with secrets I know are lurking beneath his charming facade, a man with a dark past that threatens to dictate who he will become.

And I think I love him.

I can't bring myself to tell him that. I just had the chance a moment ago when he told me he wasn't able to come tonight because he was with his brother and Carter needed him.

But he still asked if I needed anything. I could have told him I miss him. I could have messaged him more. Instead, I simply told him I would be ready for him when he wanted me.

The constant thumping in my chest gets harder and rises higher. I have to swallow it down just so I can breathe. This was never supposed to happen. How could I have fallen for a man like him?

I'm drowning in the abyss, and he's the only one there to hold me. That's how. I need to remember that.

He made it that way, didn't he?

The sound of the radiator kicking on disrupts the quiet living room. I take the moment to have a sip of tea, careful not to disturb the open book in my lap. The warmth of the mug against my lips is nothing compared to Jase's kiss.

With my eyes closed, I vow to think clearly, to step back and be smart about all of this. Even though deep inside, I know there is no way that means I could ever stay with Jase Cross, and the very thought destroys something deep inside of me. Splintering it and causing a pain that forces me to put the cup down and sink back into the sofa, covering myself with the blanket and staring at the black and white words on the page.

It all hurts when I think about leaving him.

That's how I know I've fallen.

The Coverless Book
Eighth Chapter

Jake's perspective

"Kiss me again?" Emmy's voice is soft and delicate. It fits her, but she's so much more.

"You like it when I kiss you?" I tease her and that bright pink blush rises up her cheeks.

"Shhh, she'll hear us," she says as her small hands press against my chest, pushing me to the side so she can glance past me and toward the hallway to the kitchen.

"Miss Caroline knows I kiss you." I smile as I push some strands of hair behind her ear, but it falls slowly. It should be her mother who Emmy's afraid will catch us. But her mother is never here.

"Maybe go check on her?" Emmy asks, scooting me off the chair. "See what she's doing and if we have a little more time?"

It's her elation that draws me to her. There are some people in this world who you love to see smile. It makes you warm inside and it feels like everything will be all right, if only they smile.

That's all I can think as I round the corner to the kitchen. I've only been here to Emmy's house twice, but I know the help's kitchen is through one of these two doors. I'm right on the first guess and there's Caroline, hovering over the large pot with a skinny bottle above it. Clear liquid is being poured into the steaming pot of soup.

Although I'd planned to offer to help, just so I can gauge how much time we have, my words are stolen.

The glass bottle she's holding doesn't look like it belongs in a kitchen. I feel a deep crease form between my furrowed brows and I stare for far too long as she pours more and more into the pot. She's humming as she does. A sweet tune I'm sure would lull babies to their dreams.

Emmy has soup every night. Every night the caretaker makes her soup. And Emmy stays sick, every day.

"What did you put in there?" My question comes out hard and when Miss Caroline jumps, the liquid spills over the oven and the bottle crashes onto the floor with her startled cry.

I debate on grabbing the notebook from the kitchen counter where I left it. Just so I can add to the collection of underlined sentences. I'm reading without really paying attention, just letting the time go by.

My gaze skims the page, finding four sentences underlined this time and none of the four hold any new meaning. One is the same as it's been for a while now. *I'm invincible.*

If it weren't for the distraction of this story, the suspense and the emotion, I'd feel hopeless. I'm hopeless when it comes to Jase.

If hope is a long way of saying goodbye, hopeless can

only mean one of two things. As the thought plays in my mind, my thumb brushes along my bottom lip and I stare at the page.

And that's when I see it. What I've been waiting for. What I was so sure was here.

A chill spreads across my skin as the mug slips from my hand, dropping to the floor, crashing into pieces. If the letters weren't staring right at me, I never would have seen them.

It's not the underlined sentences. *It's the lines below them.* The first letters of the sentences *beneath* the pen marks. C. R. O. S. S. She buried the message so deep, I didn't see it before.

At first it hits me she left me a message, and there's hope. And then I read the word again.

C. R. O. S. S.

"No." The word is whispered from me, but not with conscious consent. My head shakes and my fingers tremble as I stare at the evidence.

C. R. O. S. S.

She did leave a note. My blood turns to ice at the thought. Jenny left me a message in this book, and it has to do with the Cross brothers.

"No." I repeat the word as I lay the book down, although not gently, but forcefully, as if it will bite me if I hold it any longer. I nearly trip over the throw blanket in my rush to get off the sofa.

Thump, thump, thump. Ever present and ever painful, my bastard heart races inside of me.

My limbs are wobbly as I rush to the kitchen, searching for the notebook. I need to write it down. "Write it all down," I speak in hushed and rushed words as I pull open one drawer in the kitchen, jostling the pens, a pair of scissors, and papers and everything else in the junk drawer. It slams shut as I bring the notebook to my chest, ready to face the book. To face the message Jenny left me.

Knowing she wrote something about the Cross brothers.

Knowing Jase Cross lied to me.

They had something to do with her murder. Maybe even him.

Tears leak from my eyes as I stumble in the kitchen.

"No," I whisper, and force myself to stand. *It will say something else.* I tell myself it will, and the sinful whisper in my head reminds me, *Hope is a long way of saying goodbye.*

Swallowing down my heart and nerves, I push myself to stand, only to hear a creak.

Thump, goes my heart, and this time the beat comes with fear.

I couldn't have heard that right. No one is coming. No one is here, I tell myself, even though my blood still rushes inside of me, begging me to run, warning me that something's wrong, that someone's here who isn't supposed to be.

I keep silent and hear the sound of my front door.

Thump. Terror betrays my instincts. Stealing my breath and making me lightheaded.

The foyer floor creaks again and the front door closes, softly. A gentle push. A quiet one meant not to disturb.

The creaking moves closer and I listen to it with only the harsh sound of my subdued breath competing with it.

And I'm too afraid to even whisper, "Who's there?"

Jase and Bethany's book continues in … *A Single Kiss*.
Preorder now!

There are many moving parts in this world. If you haven't read Carter's saga, starting with *Merciless*, I highly suggest you do that now. His story is just as intense and a tale that will stay with me forever. I hope these words stay with you as well.

Here's to love stories keeping our hearts beating.

ABOUT THE AUTHOR

Thank you so much for reading my romances. I'm just a stay at home mom and avid reader turned author and I couldn't be happier.

I hope you love my books as much as I do!

More by Willow Winters
www.willowwinterswrites.com/books

Made in USA - North Chelmsford, MA
42111_9781795452731
12.09.2023 0520